Skip Shaughnessy

in

A Way to Escape

Skip's Action Series

Book 3

Marjorie Strebe

Published by:
Marjorie Strebe
Trenton, OH 45067

Interior Design by Marjorie Strebe
Book Cover Design by 100 Covers

Skip Shaughnessy in A Way to Escape / Marjorie Strebe
Library of Congress Control Number: 2024925398
ISBN: 979-8-9902136-2-3
Printed in the United States of America

I will say of the Lord, He is my refuge and my

fortress: my God; in Him will I trust.

Psalm 91:2

Table of Contents

1. A Set Up........................7

2. Swayed by the Rumor Tree........................15

3. The Ringing Telephone........................25

4. Condemned on Hearsay........................35

5. The Healing Truth........................41

6. A New Plan........................47

7. A Water-Filled Prison........................53

8. Taking Action........................57

9. The Worry Warriors........................65

10. Pondering Possibilities........................75

11. Ignoring the Warning........................81

12. Dropping a Clue........................91

13. Enlisting Help........................97

14. Deciphering the Clues........................103

15. The Empty Search........................111

16. The Lord's Direction........................117

17. Baiting the Trap........................125

18. A Little Detour........................133

19. A Piece of Evidence........................145

20. Looking at the Facts........................153

21. A Gathering of Evil Minds........................159

22. A Ride on Cupcake........................163

23. Caught in a Lie.................................171

24. A Hint of Animosity.........................179

25. Making Decisions............................185

26. In Need of Security.........................191

27. Strange Happenings.........................197

28. The Mysterious Voices......................207

29. New Developments..........................213

30. Stake Out.....................................219

31. Another Disappearance.....................227

32. An Escape Attempt..........................233

33. Unanswered Questions......................237

34. While Waiting for the Sheriff...............243

35. The Great Escape...........................251

36. The Hostage Dilemma.......................259

37. Fishing for Information......................265

38. The Key to Rescue..........................273

39. Following the Trail...........................279

40. The Search for Stephanie..................285

41. Returning Home.............................295

42. Wrapping up the Details.....................303

Chapter 1

A Set Up

Cruising down the deserted highway, 19-year-old Skip Shaughnessy had one prevailing thought – to get home and go to bed. From a side street, a pickup truck turned toward him, blinking on the high beams before crossing the yellow line into his lane. Was this guy drunk or just not paying attention?

With no time to think, and less than a second to react, Skip dodged the truck – and quickly. Blinded by the headlights, he couldn't escape the glaring beam. He slammed on the brakes and jerked the wheel to the right, but the pickup chased him, forcing him into a hard right to avoid a head-on collision.

Careening down the embankment, Skip plowed into the ditch. The car jolted to a sudden stop, and the tires spun. He was stuck.

Ouch. That hurt.

A Way to Escape

It was 1995, the last Friday in May. Having been released from the hospital only eight days earlier, he was still healing from some of the third-degree burns he sustained from a house fire. Although he was healing remarkably fast, he was still tender in spots.

Skip slammed the heel of his hand on the steering wheel and shot an angry glance into his rear view mirror, hoping to catch sight of some specific detail to identify the vehicle that just ran him off the road. But the truck had disappeared from view. And with his hyper-sensitivity to light, despite the protection of dark glasses, the high beams left him seeing spots. So he didn't even see the color.

"Wonderful." Skip crossed his arms over the steering wheel and rested his head. "I just wrecked Greg's car on the most deserted stretch of road between my house and Cassandra's with no way to notify anyone."

His family was out of town until Sunday, and his mom had taken the family van. So he borrowed this old jalopy from a fellow officer at the police station.

With a frustrated sigh, Skip slid from the car and climbed out of the ditch. Standing on the side of the road, he looked both directions. Five miles ahead was an all-night convenience store, while two miles back sat a tavern.

Skip groaned at the thought, but he was tired. And since the bar was much closer than the store, he turned around and started walking.

Steering back into his lane, Sam Richter laughed. It was easy to run someone off the road when they would do just about anything to avoid a collision. And after lingering at the corner for nearly ninety minutes waiting for that kid, he found it rewarding to watch the lad plow into the ditch.

Sam snatched up the receiver to his car phone which was bolted to the dash, and he hit the redial button.

"Lucky Star Tavern."

"Okay, Wayne, tell Rusty to expect Shaughnessy in about a half hour. The bar is by far the closest establishment to him."

"Sam, do you really think this will work?" asked Wayne.

"I don't know, but I've heard that Cassandra McKenzie easily jumps to conclusions, so for a hundred grand, it's worth a shot. I'll be there in two minutes." Sam hung up.

Arriving at the bar a couple minutes later, Sam pulled into the parking lot and maneuvered his white, super cab pickup truck around back. He felt certain that Skip couldn't identify it, especially after blinding him with high beams, but he didn't want to risk it.

Sam pushed through the door and headed for the bar. With a slight nod, he acknowledged Rusty O'Sheif before climbing onto a bar stool. Wayne Thomas, the bartender, poured him a drink, and Sam downed it in one swallow.

"Now this kid doesn't drink," he whispered to Wayne. "Any alcohol he consumes will affect him, so offer him a

glass of soda, *and spike it.* It's important for Cassandra
to believe that he's drinking."

After a thirty-minute hike, Skip finally reached his
destination. He stepped inside the tavern and spotted a
pay telephone just inside the door. With a sigh, he
inserted a quarter and punched in his fiancée's number.
He'd promised to call her when he got home.

Cassandra snatched up the receiver on the first ring.
"Skip?"

"Yeah, it's me."

"I'm glad you called. I was starting to get worried."

"Well ... um ... I'm not calling from home. Some idiot
ran me off the road, and the car's in a ditch. I won't get
home until real late, and I didn't want you to worry."

"Where are you calling from? My mom and I will
come get you."

"Thanks, Cassie, but I have to call Greg about his car,
and I know that he'll come for it tonight, so I'll catch a
ride with him."

"Call me the moment you get home, no matter how
late it is."

"Cassandra, you're as bad as my mother. I'll call you
when I get home. Bye-bye."

He disconnected the call and dropped another quarter
into the coin slot.

Sam leaned across the bar and lowered his voice. "Okay, Wayne. That's him. You know what to do."

Wayne's eyes widened. "My gosh, Sammy. He's just a teenager. He's not old enough to drink."

"Shh. Just give it to him."

Wayne filled a glass with Pepsi and added something a lot stronger. The moment Skip hung up, Wayne handed him the glass. "Here, son. Thought you might be thirsty after that long hike."

Sam cringed. That comment would surely throw suspicion onto Wayne.

Skip's shaded eyes narrowed. "Long hike?"

"Uh, yeah. I overheard you on the phone."

It appeared to Sam that the boy didn't believe Wayne and for good reason. While on the phone, he'd kept his voice soft enough that they couldn't hear him from across the room. "Would you like it?"

Skip's eyes shifted from Wayne to the glass. "What is it?"

"Pepsi."

He must have been thirsty because he received the glass.

"Thank you." Skip took one sip and gagged, making a face like he'd just ingested castor oil. "What's in this?"

"N-n-nothing. Let me get you another one."

"No, thank you." Skip set down the glass and headed out the door, tripping over a crumpled doormat at the entrance.

Sam motioned to Rusty. Then he turned back to Wayne. "When are you going to learn how to spike a drink?"

The door hissed shut, and Rusty rose from his chair. "I have to make a phone call," he told his girlfriend. "Wait here." Hustling over to the phone, he snatched up the receiver, dropped in a quarter and punched his home phone number.

"Hello?"

"Linda, guess who came into the bar." Before his sister answered, he blurted it out. "Skip Shaughnessy."

"*You're kidding.* Was he drinking?"

"It looked like it. Wayne handed him a glass of something."

"Is he still there?"

"No, but he tripped on his way out the door and almost fell."

Linda gasped. "He was drunk? Poor Cassandra. I'd better call her. I'll bet she doesn't know. Thanks for calling, Rusty."

Linda hung up the phone and dialed Cassandra's number.

"Hello?"

"Cassandra, are you sitting down? Skip just staggered out of the bar."

"Bar?" repeated Cassandra. "He just called, but he didn't say he was at a bar.

"Well, he was." Linda could hardly contain her excitement at this juicy bit of gossip.

"I don't believe that. First of all, Skip doesn't drink. Are you talking about Skip Shaughnessy?"

"Of course. But if you don't believe me, ask him and see what he says."

"I'll do that. Bye, Linda."

Linda hung up the phone and dialed another number. "Jill, guess who staggered out of the bar tonight. *Skip Shaughnessy.*"

Jill gasped. "You're kidding. Was he alone"

"Probably not. I would imagine that he took a girl with him. My brother always takes a girl to the bar with him."

"Poor Cassandra. Does she know?"

"Yeah," replied Linda. "I just called her. Remember to pray for her."

"You bet. Thanks for telling me, Linda."

Jill hung up the phone and dialed another number. "Julie, guess what? Skip Shaughnessy was in the bar tonight."

Julie gasped. "You're not serious. Skip? In the bar? Where did you hear this?"

"Linda just phoned me. She saw him stagger out, and she thinks he was with another girl," said Jill.

"Boy, I have a hard time believing that, but Linda is a very reliable source. Has anyone called Cassandra?"

"Linda called her. Remember her in your prayers tonight."

"You bet. Thanks for calling, Jill. Bye."

Thoughtfully, Julie replaced the receiver. *Skip at a bar? That's the news of the century.* She snatched up the receiver again. "Carol, we need to pray for Cassandra."

"What's happening with Cassandra?"

"Jill just phoned me. Skip Shaughnessy was in a bar tonight with another girl, and he was drunk."

"Poor Cassandra. I always liked Skip, too – *the bum.* How did Jill know this? Did she see him?"

"No. Linda saw him. Then Linda phoned Jill, and Jill called me," said Julie.

"Has anyone called Cassandra?"

"Yeah, Linda called her. Just pray for her, okay?"

Chapter 2

Swayed by the Rumor Tree

Wearing down fast, Skip trudged back to the car and climbed onto the back of it to sit down. A few minutes later, a patrol car pulled onto the shoulder of the road and on went the flashing lights. Officer Charlie Curtis slid out of the car with his clipboard and trotted down the steep grassy slope.

"Hey, Skip, what happened?"

"Some idiot ran me off the road."

"Did you get a good look at the car? Make? Model? Color? License?"

"I think it was a pickup truck."

"You think?" Curtis raised an eyebrow. "You're not sure?"

"Nope."

"You're supposed to be a trained observer. Weren't you paying attention?"

"For your information, the instant he turned the corner, he blinded me with his brights. And I was too busy trying to avoid a head-on collision to worry about the make and model of his vehicle, especially since he seemed bent on crashing into me head on."

"Were his headlights already on bright when he turned toward you, or did he deliberately switch them to high beams?"

"It was deliberate, all right. Hey, what are you doing here, anyway? I didn't call the police."

"Greg called and sent us out here to take a report." Charlie took down what information he could and left.

Skip waited another hour for Greg to arrive. Finally, a yellow tow truck coasted onto the shoulder of the road.

"Hey, Skippy Peanut Butter," called Greg through the open cab window. "Glad to see that you weren't hurt."

Skip breathed a sigh of relief. At least Greg didn't sound angry with him for landing in the ditch.

Greg hopped out the passenger door of the tow truck and trotted down the hill to examine his car for damage. "Did you catch the license number of the guy who ran you off the road?"

"Unfortunately, no."

It took much longer than Skip anticipated for them to get the car out of the ditch and back onto the blacktop.

Greg slid behind the steering wheel and cranked up the engine, beckoning for Skip to join him.

"Jump in, and I'll run you home." Greg closed his car door and rolled down his window to talk to the tow truck driver. "Thanks, Vince. I appreciate it."

"Forget it," said Vince. "I owed you anyway."

With a wave, Greg accelerated onto the road, and Skip rattled off his address.

"I didn't realize you lived so far from the station," said Greg. "How long does it take you to get to work?"

"Twenty five minutes." Setting his elbow on the window ledge, Skip propped his head on his hand.

Boy, did I blow it.

A month shy of his twentieth birthday, he'd been with the Forest Valley, Wyoming, Police Department for nearly two years. Skip's best friend, Johnny Marshall, a lieutenant with the department, had approached Chief Clark during Skip's senior year of high school. He wanted to know if there was any way they could make an exception regarding the age requirement and allow his young friend to join the department upon his high school graduation.

Chief Clark had seen incredible potential in Skip. So the chief had petitioned the governor to grant special approval to accept a student right out of high school, allowing him to join two years younger than the minimum age requirement.

Finally accepted as part of the department by the other officers, Skip feared that this incident would now brand him as irresponsible.

With his right hand on the wheel and his left arm resting comfortably on his open window, Greg glanced over at him and back at the road. "You okay?"

"I suppose. I'm really sorry about your car. I'll pay for the damage."

"That little scrape on the right fender? Skip, don't worry about the car. It's replaceable. You are not."

By the time Skip walked through his front door, it was well past midnight, and he could hardly keep his eyes open. But Cassandra would be sitting by the telephone, waiting for his call.

Trudging into the kitchen, he grabbed the receiver and dialed her number. Halfway into the first ring Cassandra's agitated voice shot over the line, so Skip suspected that she was waiting by the phone.

"Skip, is that you?"

"Yeah, Cassie. I'm home."

"What a relief to hear your voice. I was so worried. Did you stop by the bar on your way home?"

"No. After I got run off the road, I hiked back to the nearest establishment to use the telephone. That happened to be a bar."

"Is that all you did? Use the telephone? Because Linda phoned me and said she saw you stagger out."

"I didn't stagger. I tripped over a crumpled mat in the doorway. You know that I never touch alcohol."

Cassandra breathed a sigh. "I know, but it's good to hear you say it. I'm sorry for questioning your Christian standards. Can you come over tomorrow?"

"I have no way. I'm stranded without a car."

"I understand. See you next week then."

"Bye, Cassandra." Skip turned off the light and went to bed.

With his mom and four young sisters out of town, Skip awoke to an unbelievably quiet house. Not used to this kind of solitude and silence, he wanted to jump into his mom's van and go see Cassandra. Unfortunately, he was stranded without a vehicle. So it was a good thing he didn't have to work today.

He was still on administrative leave for shooting a warehouse burglary suspect two weeks ago while on an undercover assignment for the police department. Skip only returned fire when the man shot at him, but he killed the suspect. And until the Grand Jury determined the shooting was justifiable, he couldn't return to work. That ruling could come down this week. But more than likely, he won't be cleared to return to work for another month.

Skip opened several ground-floor windows to freshen the house with the warm breeze. This would be a good day to resume his search for the Colorado Rockies autographed baseball that his dad had. Surely his mom wouldn't give away something that he valued so highly. After all, she kept everything.

"Lord, help me find that baseball. It was my dad's, and I know he would want me to have it."

Wandering from room to room, Skip ran through a mental checklist of every place he'd already looked. He hadn't yet searched the basement, and since a ball like that meant nothing to his mother, he could see her tossing it down there. But that room was such a disaster, he kept the door locked to keep Scooter or Suzi from wandering downstairs and getting hurt.

Skip plucked the set of keys from the hook in the kitchen, inserted the shiny gold-colored key into the lock, and opened the basement door. Jiggling the key, he worked to free it from the lock.

"I'll get it later."

Leaving the keys dangling from the lock, he trotted down the stairs to the massive underground room. Skip rummaged through the basement clutter, hunting through piles of boxes in the dim light.

"What's this?" Picking up a scrapbook, he blew the dust off the cover and sat down to look through it. He'd never seen these pictures and newspaper clippings before. According to the date, his mother started this scrapbook of his father's police career before he was born. The book documented his entire police career through photographs, letters, and newspaper articles, until his death, four years ago.

Skip turned the pages slowly, reading each letter and article, captivated by this glimpse into his father's life. Pausing, he studied a black and white glossy of his uniformed father posing proudly in front of the police department with a small baby in his arms. Gently popping the over sized picture out of the four corners, he turned it over to read the inscription on the back, written in his mother's familiar handwriting. *My handsome Stevie, holding our beautiful son.*

"I wonder why my mom never showed me this book."

Bang!

Skip jumped to his feet when the basement door slammed shut. Setting aside the book, he bounded up the stairs to the door. It was locked. He rattled it, attempting to force it open.

"Wonderful. I'm locked in."

With the telephone receiver to her ear, Cassandra gasped at the allegation. "No, no, Cathy. You must have seen someone else. Skip wouldn't be running around on me."

"You know, I didn't see him. That's what Teri said."

"Teri?"

"Yeah, according to Teri, Linda saw him. Then she told Jill, and Jill phoned Julie. Julie called Carol. Carol called Angela. And Angela told Teri. Then Teri called me."

"You're kidding."

"Would I lie to you?"

"Well, to the best of my knowledge you never have. Is it possible you made a mistake? I can't imagine Skip doing such a thing."

"I didn't make a mistake. I know what Teri told me, but I suppose Teri could have gotten the story wrong."

Teri didn't get the story wrong, thought Cassandra. *'Cause that's exactly what Linda told me, except she failed to mention the girl.*

Choking down a sob, she bid Cathy good-bye and hung up the phone.

"What was that all about?" asked Anita McKenzie, Cassandra's mother.

"Linda saw Skip at a bar with another girl last night, and he'd been drinking." Angry tears coursed down her cheeks.

"Skip? At a bar? Come on, Cassandra, get real."

"He stopped by a bar last night. I asked him."

"What was he doing there?"

"He said he was using the telephone."

"I take it, you don't believe him."

Cassandra dried her eyes and reached for the telephone receiver. "I'm gonna call Linda and find out why she didn't tell me about that other girl."

Anita placed her hand on Cassandra's, preventing her daughter from picking up the telephone receiver. "No, you're not. The only person you should talk to about this is Skip. These girls are professional gossips, spreading discord that is harming your relationship with him. Now call Skip, and get the facts. Then drop this nonsense, and don't listen to any more gossip."

"Okay." Cassandra picked up the phone and dialed Skip's number. The phone just rang. "He's not home," she said indignantly.

"Maybe he had somewhere to go."

"Maybe he did, but he told me that he'd be home all day because he was stranded without a car. *Obviously, he's not.*"

Chapter 3

The Ringing Telephone

Skip threw his weight against the basement door, trying to force it open, but to no avail. With the basement steps leading right up to the door, he couldn't get the thrust or leverage he needed to kick it open. Leaning against the door, he sighed and slid down to the top step, listening to the phone ring.

"I wonder who that is." The phone rang eight times. "It's probably Mom, calling to tell me they won't be home until Tuesday. Just my luck. I could be locked down here for days."

Since he was on administrative leave, no one from the station would even miss him, which meant that no one would come looking for him. He was on his own.

Skip considered another means of escape. "The window."

A Way to Escape

Bounding down the steps, he waded through the clutter to the far wall, looking up at the window. It was high, and it wasn't very big. Would he be able to climb up there and crawl through?

Skip moved a small lopsided bookcase, books and all, and set it against the wall under the window. The bookshelf wobbled when he climbed onto it. Barely able to reach the window latch, he needed a little more elevation, so he jumped down and stacked some heavy books on top of the bookshelf to stand on.

The phone rang again, and Skip looked toward the closed basement door. This time it rang ten times. The call must be important because the caller was persistent. Unfortunately, Skip forgot to turn on the answering machine.

Climbing onto the wobbly bookcase, he stepped onto the books. Finally high enough to reach the window latch, he unlocked the window and tried to push it open, but it didn't budge. He pounded on the top of the window ledge, attempting to jar the window loose. Then he remembered why it wouldn't open.

The month before his dad died, he'd gotten drafted to help with some painting and repairs around the house. In a hurry to complete the chore he'd been assigned, he ignored his dad's instructions and painted the basement windows shut, rationalizing that it didn't matter since they never opened those windows anyway.

Frustrated with himself for disregarding his dad, Skip whammed the top of the window with the heel of his hand. Pursing his lips, he hammered it again. But instead of opening the window, the particleboard beneath his feet splintered under his weight. He tumbled to the concrete floor, scraping his arm on a jagged fragment of the bookcase and smacking his head. Books lay scattered everywhere.

"Ouch." Skip sat up and rubbed his head. "That hurt."

Blood trickled down his arm. After examining the deep scratch that stretched from his elbow to his wrist, he surveyed the massive clutter for a clean rag to wrap around his arm. "What else could possibly go wrong?"

The phone rang again.

Skip stumbled over a jumble of long-forgotten toys to the pile of baby clothes in the corner and snatched up an old burp cloth. He shook out the dust, folded it lengthwise, and covered the scrape on his arm. Rummaging through miscellaneous baby items, he searched for something to secure it to his arm.

"Ah, baby headbands." He remembered how pretty they made his baby sisters look. He found a couple the right size and slid them onto his arm to hold the make-shift dressing in place, wincing from the throbbing pain.

"Lord Jesus, how am I going to get out of here?" Skip dropped onto the piles of clothes that practically covered the floor. With a yawn, he lay down and closed his eyes. Nestled comfortably in the soft material that surrounded him, he drifted to sleep.

Cassandra hung up the phone and folded her arms on the table, laying her head down.

"Still no answer?" Anita rested her hand on her daughter's shoulder.

"No."

"Well, Melanie and I are going shopping. Why don't you come with us and try again when we get back."

"Thanks, Mom. I don't feel like going anywhere. I think I'll stay home."

"Okay, dear. But don't be calling all your friends. You should talk to Skip."

"He lied to me." Tears streamed down her cheeks.

"Cassandra, you don't have all the answers. Maybe he had an emergency and had to leave. Give him the benefit of the doubt."

"I'm trying, but it's awfully hard."

"And it gets harder every time you listen to one of your friends. They are gossiping, Cassandra. They are spreading rumors that you have yet to confirm."

Not exactly, thought Cassandra. Linda informed her that Skip was at a bar, and he admitted it, so it wasn't a rumor. He was really there, although he claimed that he only used the telephone. And she believed him until word reached her that he'd been seen with another girl and was drunk. That explained why it took him almost four hours to get home after he dropped her off.

Skip slept for two hours. When he awoke, his thoughts flew to his dad's tools. He bolted upright.

"A hammer."

With a frown, he slowly rose to his feet, surveying the disaster that surrounded him. A sense of dread overwhelmed him. It could take him days to find a hammer in this mess.

But where do I begin my search? Look at this mess, Lord. I had no idea that my well-being could be compromised by such disorder. My mother's been after me for months to clean up this basement. I always have an excuse why I can't do it. I shall start this project as soon as possible. Maybe Cassandra will help me.

Skip scanned the room. Wading through the disarray of miscellaneous objects, he reached for a blanket and yanked it away from the pile that it covered.

"Tool boxes. Thank you, Lord."

He popped the latch and opened the lid. Skip grinned. There sat his prized baseball, encased in a thin plastic cube. He'd been praying for months that God would show him where to look. And yet, the first time he prayed about it, his mother asked him to clean up the basement.

Skip picked up the cube, turning it over in his hands. Since he hadn't made time to clean up the basement for his mother, God locked him down there long enough for him to see the need to restore order, and he found his baseball in the process.

With a contented sigh, he set down the cube and grabbed the hammer and a small flathead screwdriver.

A Way to Escape

Stepping over things, he trotted up the stairs to the locked door, inserted the tiny screwdriver into the lock, and struck the handle with the hammer, pounding it in. With a jingle, his keys fell to the floor. He tried the doorknob, but it was still locked, so he turned the screwdriver handle like a key, but the lock didn't give. Taking the hammer once more, Skip pounded the screwdriver in again.

Pop. He'd broken the lock.

Breathing a sigh of relief, he pushed open the door and stepped into the kitchen.

"That was nerve-wracking. I hope I never go through anything like that again."

After his confinement in the dimly-lit basement, the sudden bright light made him squint, despite wearing dark glasses. The phone rang again, and Skip picked it up.

"Hello?"

"Hi, Skip, this is Mom. I haven't talked to you for two days, so I'm calling to check on you. Is everything all right?"

Oh, sure. I got run off the road last night. I'm stranded without a car. I locked myself down in the basement. I fell through a bookcase, banged my head, and scraped my arm. And I just broke the lock on the basement door. Things couldn't possibly be better.

"Skip?"

"Mom, are you worried that I'm home alone?" Skip glanced at his throbbing arm. "Don't you trust me to take care of myself?"

"Of course, I do. But I still like to hear your voice and know that you're safe."

"What would you have done if the phone just rang, and I didn't answer it?"

"I would have called Johnny and asked him to check on you."

Skip grinned. Maybe he wouldn't have been locked down in the basement all weekend.

"Incidentally, I'm calling to let you know that the girls miss you tremendously, especially Stephanie, so we're coming home a day early."

"Okay, Mom. I'll see you tomorrow afternoon." Skip hung up, and the phone promptly rang again.

That couldn't possibly be his mother. He gazed uncertainly at the ringing telephone, afraid his mother had realized that he sidestepped her question. On the fourth ring, he picked it up.

"H-hello?"

"Where have you been?" demanded Cassandra. "I've been trying to reach you all day."

Skip swallowed hard. Cassandra would laugh at him if she knew that he'd accidentally locked himself in the basement.

"I'm sorry, Cassandra. I wasn't able to get to the phone."

"Why not?"

"Well, um, I just wasn't. That's all."

"Where did you go, Skip?"

"No place. I don't have a car. What's with you, anyway? You're not upset that I didn't answer the phone. There's something else bothering you. What is it?"

"Look, just give me the whole story about last night."

Skip paused. "I did. What else is there to tell?"

"That's your story then?"

"It's the only one I've got. I don't know what you want to hear."

"The truth." With that, she hung up.

Skip stood stunned. She just accused him of lying. To say the least, the last twenty-four hours had been horrendous, and now this. He'd call her back and find out what was really bothering her. Hopefully, he could straighten out any misunderstanding before it got worse.

Skip punched in Cassandra's number, but her phone just rang. With a sigh, he disconnected the call and trotted up the steps to the bathroom to take care of his arm.

After removing the soft rag, he gently washed his arm in cool water and poured hydrogen peroxide over the scrape. The scratch was deep, but there was nothing more he could do for it. He patted his arm dry and trotted down the stairs to fix himself a bite to eat.

Skip phoned Cassandra several times throughout the day and left two or three messages on the recorder. No one answered the phone, and Cassandra had yet to call him back. With each unanswered phone call he made, his apprehension grew. By evening, Skip knew that if he didn't turn to the Lord for strength and support, he wouldn't sleep that night, so he reached for his Bible. After reading for an hour, he bowed his head in prayer.

Finally closing his Bible, Skip stood, gazing down at the silent telephone. Why wouldn't Cassandra talk to him? He paced the room, debating whether he should phone her again. He'd stayed by the phone all day, waiting for her return call. Wringing his hands, he reached for the phone, hurriedly dialing her number once more. No answer.

"I need some fresh air. I think I'll go for a walk."

Skip gazed down at his scraped arm. Although it was a warm evening, he slipped on a long-sleeve shirt and pulled his ball cap down far enough to hide the bruise on his forehead. Snatching up his keys and jacket, he left the house.

Chapter 4

Condemned on Hearsay

Standing at the dining room table, Cassandra blinked back tears and scooped the leftover beans from the black pot into a seal-tight container.

Why would Skip do such a thing to her? Then to lie about it. He acted so innocent – like he had no idea what she was talking about.

For a moment, Cassandra wondered if it could possibly be a misunderstanding. She recalled the time that she had accused him of using her younger sister. It had infuriated her to think that Skip had arranged twenty-four hour police surveillance on Melanie to catch the ring leader of the high school drug gang. As it turned out, because of her involvement with that drug dealer, Melanie had gotten herself in deep, and that surveillance had saved her life. Needless to say, Cassandra had felt like a fool for falsely accusing Skip.

But this is different, she thought. *Linda saw him at a bar with another girl. She saw him, and he won't even admit it.*

Stacking the dirty dinner dishes, she carried them into the kitchen and placed them in the hot, soapy water for her sister to wash. Her mother trailed her into the kitchen.

"Cassandra, have you talked to Skip, yet?"

I don't want to talk to him. Shaking her head in frustration. Cassandra turned away to keep her mother from seeing the angry tears.

"Why don't you call him again? It's almost nine o'clock. Surely, he's home by now."

Cassandra forced a smile and reached for the receiver, punching in his number. She was only doing this to please her mother. She feared that Skip would answer the phone, and she'd have no choice but talk to him. Then she thought of how pleasant it would be to hear his voice and what if, by some miracle, this rumor could be dispelled by a simple phone call.

The phone just rang.

The cool breeze felt good. Strolling around the block, Skip gazed up at the trillions of glittering stars that dotted the sky like white paint spatters on a black surface. It reminded him that he served a God bigger than the universe itself. The night was clear and the moon full, giving him the light needed to navigate down a dark street.

He talked to God as he walked, filling the void in his heart. Nothing eased his loneliness like spending time with God. Arriving back at his house, Skip lay down on the front lawn. He wasn't ready to go back inside, where the walls seemed to close in on him with a continuous reminder of his strained relationship with Cassandra.

Skip folded his hands underneath his head and stared into space, counting stars. The next thing he knew, he felt a gentle shake.

"Hey, Skip, are you all right?"

"Hm?" Skip's eyes fluttered open and he blinked, trying to focus on the police officer squatting beside him. He slowly sat up. "Pete, what time is it?" Removing his glasses, Skip rubbed his eyes.

"It's almost two o'clock," said Officer Pete Kalen.

"In the morning?"

"Yep. Why don't you go in, and go to bed? You'll sleep better."

With a yawn, Skip stumbled to his feet. "Goodnight, Pete."

Skip knew that he should call someone to pick him up for church. But he felt the need to be alone with God. So he chose to have private devotions, spending his morning with God in prayer and in the Bible.

The day dragged. He couldn't wait for his mother to get home with the van, yet he dreaded it. He had to go see Cassandra, to find out what had come between them. And he feared her reaction. With turmoil churning within him, he couldn't eat.

Shortly before sunset, his mom and little sisters arrived home. The four blond-haired girls, ranging in age from three to nine, burst through the door and mobbed him. Caught off guard, Skip tumbled to the linoleum, and the girls piled into his lap, inundating him with hugs and kisses. For a moment, he forgot his troubles with Cassandra.

"We missed you." cried little Suzi, soon to be five years old. She planted her lips against his cheek. "Did you miss us?"

"I sure did, darling."

"Skip, why didn't you come with us?" asked seven-year-old Sandy.

"Not enough room in the van. Did you pack lots of toys?"

"Uh-huh." All the girls nodded.

"See? There was no room for me." Skip crawled out from under his sisters and got to his feet, turning to his mother as she entered the house with an armload. "Mom, do you mind if I run over to Cassandra's house for a little awhile?"

Dumping things on the sofa, Erin embraced and kissed him. "Of course not. You stay as long as you'd like."

"Can we go, Skip?" chimed his little sisters.

"Not this time, I'm afraid. But you can help me unload the van for Mom."

With help from the girls, Skip unloaded Erin's mint green minivan before heading across town to Cassandra's house.

Sitting on her bed, Cassandra sobbed at the thought of losing Skip to another woman.

"You want to talk about it?" Anita dropped onto the bed beside her daughter, pulling her into a warm hug.

Cassandra shook her head. "He lied to me, Mom. He was out with another girl yesterday, too."

"How do you know that? Cassandra, you are drawing conclusions based on gossip. Now, you have to talk to Skip."

"I will. I'll call off our engagement."

"That's your right, but you are making a mistake by acting so hastily."

Jerking away from her mother, Cassandra stared at her. She couldn't believe it. Her mother just sided with Skip. "You don't believe any of it. Do you?"

"No, I don't. Skip is human, Cassandra, and he could be guilty. But I won't believe it unless I see it or he admits it. He's honest, reliable, trustworthy, and *he doesn't lie.* If he said that he only used the telephone and left, I believe him. Why don't you?"

Just then, Melanie barged in. "Sorry to interrupt, but ..."

"Get out."

"Cassandra!" gasped her mother.

"I'm sorry, Cassandra. But I just thought you might ..."

Cassandra shoved her sister into the hall and shut the door in her face.

Melanie shouted through the closed door. "... like to know that Skip is at the door."

"Good," said Anita. Opening the door, she spoke to her younger daughter. "Invite him in."

Cassandra gasped. *No. I don't want to see him.*

"I did, but he said he'd wait outside. He's standing on the front porch, waiting for Cassandra to come out."

Turning away, Cassandra mumbled. "I ... I'd rather not talk to him right now."

"Why not?" demanded her mother. "You've been trying to reach him for two days in order to ask him about these rumors. How come you don't want to see him now?"

"I just don't. That's all."

"Fine. Then *you* go tell him. Go look him right in the eye, and tell him that you're calling off your engagement based on a lie."

"It's not a lie," cried Cassandra.

"How do you know? You aren't the slightest bit interested in talking to Skip and hearing the truth."

Chapter 5

The Healing Truth

Cramming his hands into his pockets, Skip studied the porch step and shuffled his feet. Melanie had left the front door standing open, and the living room light shined through the glass storm door. Watching for Cassandra, Skip hoped to see her bound down the stairs toward the door, excited to see him.

He glanced at his watch and sighed. That wasn't going to happen. He'd been waiting at the door for nearly six minutes. She obviously didn't want to see him. Maybe he should take the hint and leave. Skip turned his back to the door and gazed up at the night sky.

The weather forecast is predicting severe thunderstorms tonight. If I leave now, I should get home before they hit.

At the sound of the storm door opening, Skip spun around.

"Hi, Skip," said Cassandra softly. "Come in."

Skip bit back his fear and shuffled his feet nervously. "No, thank you, Cassandra. I was hoping you'd take a walk with me."

"It looks like it's going to rain."

"Yeah, but it hasn't started yet. We need to talk."

"I know." Cassandra stepped outside and closed the door behind her. "What do you want to talk about?"

Skip raised an eyebrow. He didn't know. He wanted to discuss whatever was eating at Cassandra. She was mad at him about something.

"Cassie, I'm sorry for not being available to take your phone call yesterday. What did you want to talk to me about?"

"I'll tell you. But first, I want some answers from you. Who were you with at the bar on Friday night?"

Skip cringed. How could he have put himself into such a position? Now he understood why the Bible said to avoid even the *appearance* of evil. Someone saw him leave an establishment he never should have entered in the first place. That got people gossiping, and gossip is always destructive. Regardless, he and Cassandra already had this conversation.

"I told you. I walked to the bar to use the telephone. I went there because I was exhausted, and it was three miles closer than the convenience store. Don't you believe me?"

"I did, until I heard that Linda saw you leaving the bar with another girl."

"She couldn't have."

"Why not?"

"Because I was alone."

"Then why would she say such a thing if it's not true?"

Skip shrugged. "I don't know why others lie or gossip or spread rumors. But I'm telling you, I wasn't with any other girl, and I wasn't drinking. I used the telephone and left."

"Then why did you lie to me? Where did you go on Saturday?"

Skip sighed and shook his head. "I didn't lie to you. I didn't go anywhere. I was home all day."

"Then why didn't you answer the phone?"

"Cassandra, why don't you believe me? I've never given you a reason to suspect me of lying."

"I want to believe you, Skip. Really, I do. It's just that ..." Cassandra choked on her words. "... Linda said she saw you at the bar with another girl and that you were drunk. Cathy called and told me the same thing. Then you didn't get home until almost one when you should have been home by nine thirty. You told me you'd be home all day on Saturday, but I couldn't reach you. That led me to believe that everything they said was true and that you really were seeing another girl, and that's why you weren't home." Cassandra burst into tears.

"Cassie, I'm sorry." Skip embraced her. "Don't cry."

"Where were you yesterday, Skip? Why didn't you answer the phone all day? I tried to call you again at nine o'clock, and you weren't there."

"I went for a walk last night. You must have called while I was out."

"What about the rest of the day?"

Skip slid his hands into his pockets and shuffled his feet. "Promise you won't laugh? I, um, accidentally locked myself down in the basement."

"You did what?"

"Shh." Skip lowered his voice. "I got locked in the basement. It probably wouldn't have taken me so long to get the door open, but I was still worn out from the night before. I lay down for a minute and fell asleep. I slept for about two hours."

Cassandra cocked her head. "How did you get out?"

"I found some of my dad's tools and busted the lock on the door. Did you go to church this morning?"

Cassandra shook her head. "I couldn't bear to face you after all the rumors I'd heard. You didn't go, either?"

"I had no way."

"Why are you wearing a long sleeve shirt on such a warm evening?"

"I fell in one of my failed-escape attempts." Skip unbuttoned his cuff and rolled up his sleeve. "I scratched my arm on a jagged corner of the bookcase that I broke when I fell, and I hit my head on the concrete floor."

"You hit your head?" Cassandra reached up and removed his ball cap. "Whoa, you weren't kidding. Skip, I apologize for listening to gossip and doubting you."

"I appreciate that. You want to go for a drive with me?"

"Sure. Where are we going?"

"Linda's house." Taking his cap from Cassandra, he slipped it back on his head. "I assume you know where she lives."

"Yes."

What a relief. This situation was resolved. Now he had to confront Linda and to hopefully stop her from further damaging his reputation by setting the record straight.

Glancing up at the sky, Skip grasped her hand and hurried her toward home. Soft raindrops sprinkled his glasses, and the wind had picked up. In addition, he heard thunder in the distance. A storm was definitely heading their way.

Reaching the house, Cassandra dashed in to tell her mother where they were going. Skip jumped behind the wheel of the van and cranked the engine. A moment later, Cassandra slid in beside him, and they took off for Linda's house, which Skip discovered was a mere three blocks away. If the weather hadn't threatened to storm, they would have walked the distance.

Pulling up to the curb in front of Linda's house, Skip and Cassandra slid from the van and hiked up the front walk, rapping sharply on the door.

"What do I say?" whispered Cassandra.

"Let me do the talking."

Chapter 6

A New Plan

The door swung open, and a man stuck his head out. "Yeah? What do you want?"

Skip studied him for a moment. The guy looked vaguely familiar. "Is Linda here?"

"Um, yeah. Wait here." He closed the door on them.

Trying to remember where he'd seen that man, Skip gazed out at the rain, starting to fall. Fortunately, the porch had an overhanging roof, keeping him and Cassandra out of the weather.

A moment later, Linda opened the door. Smiling nervously at Cassandra, she joined them on the front step. "Hi, S-Skip."

"Hello, Linda. I've gotten wind of a nasty rumor that I thought you could help me clear up."

"What's that?"

"I understand that you saw me with another girl, drunk, leaving the bar."

"Me?" gasped Linda. "I've never even seen you *near* a bar. My brother called and told me that *he* saw you in the bar."

Skip raised an eyebrow. *Oh, yeah. I remember now. He was sitting in the bar last night.* "Then he can also tell you that I was alone, and I only used the telephone."

Linda's expression turned to shock, and she yelled back into the house. "Hey, Rusty, is that true?"

"What?"

Linda disappeared inside the house, slamming the storm door shut behind her, but leaving the front door standing wide open.

Skip and Cassandra exchanged glances, but neither spoke. Lightning streaked across the sky, followed a few seconds later by a distant rumble of thunder. A moment later, Linda stepped back outside, her face reddened with embarrassment.

"Skip, I'm sorry. I ... I don't know what to say."

"An apology is a good start. After that you can call your gossip grapevine, and set the record straight."

"Sure."

"I appreciate it." Skip and Cassandra dashed through the heavy rain and scrambled into the van.

"You think she'll do it?" Cassandra closed her door.

"Yeah, I do." Skip started the vehicle. "But it won't make a difference."

"What do you mean, it won't make a difference."

"The damage is done." Backing out of the driveway, Skip drove through the rainstorm, heading back to Cassandra's house. "Thanks to Rusty and Linda, I've been branded with a reputation as a liar, a drunk, and a cheat. I'm sure that some people will be glad to hear it was a mistake, but most won't believe it. That's just how people are, I'm afraid."

"Skip, I'm sorry. I feel so responsible."

"Why? It wasn't your fault." Skip pulled into Cassandra's driveway and let the van idle while they finished talking.

"I know. I just wish I'd stood by you from the start and not allowed myself to be swayed by lies, and believe them too."

"Me, too."

"I'm sorry, Skip. I won't listen to any more rumors. Can you stay and visit?"

Skip glanced at his watch and shook his head. "It's eight thirty. I'd better get home or my mom will worry about me."

"Call her from my house."

His heart skipped a beat. "Well, I think she might want to see me tonight, but ..." Boy, did he want to accept her invitation. "Okay."

Skip switched off the van and pocketed his keys.

"Ready? Go." Throwing their doors open at the same time, they dashed through the pouring rain into Cassandra's house. A sudden clash of thunder startled them, and they both jumped.

The minute Skip and Cassandra left his house, Rusty called Sam. "It didn't work. That boy's good. He was just here – *with Cassandra.* And we had no choice but tell her the truth."

Sam heaved a sigh. "Okay. Scrap plan 'A.' We'll think of something else." Sam paused, obviously in thought. "It's time to put the physical screws to that kid, something that'll scare him so badly that *he'll* call off their engagement."

Rusty grinned. He liked the sound of it all ready. "What have you got in mind?"

Pushing the door shut, Skip removed his cap, holding it loosely in his right hand.

"I'm glad you can stay for awhile." Cassandra grasped his left hand and took his ball cap from him, plopping it on her head.

Skip gazed at her. With long, auburn hair flowing out from under his ball cap and her big brown eyes tearing up, Skip knew that this had been a hard day for her, as well. And boy, did she look good in his ball cap, but then, Cassandra looked good no matter what she wore.

"Hello, Skip." Anita greeted him with a smile. "You look a little water logged. You want some cocoa?"

"Yes, ma'am. Thank you."

While Anita prepared him a mug of hot chocolate, Skip phoned his mother.

During Skip's visit, the weather turned fierce and windy. Every few seconds lightning flashed across the sky, followed by deafening clashes of thunder. The rampaging rain beat against the windows like stinging hail pellets. Promptly at nine thirty, Skip prepared to leave.

"Don't go, yet," said Cassandra. "The weather is really bad tonight. You'll get soaked before you make it to the van."

"I know, but right now, my mother is anxiously waiting for me, and she won't go to bed until I get home. Besides, I'm starved. I haven't eaten today."

"Why didn't you say something? We'd have fed you."

"Cassandra, it's not polite to go into someone's house and ask for something to eat. I'll be fine. I'll eat when I get home."

"Drive carefully, Skip. Call me as soon as you get home, so I know you got there safely."

"Okay." Gently removing his cap from her head, he put it on and pulled down the brim. Skip dashed out the door and jumped behind the wheel of his mother's van. He cranked the engine and waved at Cassandra as he slowly backed out of her driveway.

The howling storm limited his visibility and forced him to slow down considerably. Knowing it would take him twice as long to get home, he hoped that Cassandra would allow for extra driving time. Halfway home, he heard movement directly behind him.

Chapter 7

A Water-Filled Prison

Rusty crouched on the floor of the back seat of Shaughnessy's van, his Taurus thirty-two in the palm of his hand. One bullet would eliminate this problem, but Sam gave him strict orders not to hurt the kid. Shifting his weight to the seat, he saw Skip tense and glance toward his rear view mirror.

"Keep your eyes on the road." Rusty nudged him with the barrel of the gun. "Drive until I say stop, and don't give me a reason to pull the trigger."

"Don't do this, Rusty. Kidnapping at gunpoint is a felony, accompanied by serious jail time."

Great. Shaughnessy recognized his voice and knew his name. Undoubtedly, he knew that Rusty was Linda's brother, which meant that Skip could identify him. Rusty frowned. He couldn't let that boy detect that his keen observation surprised him.

"If you value your life, you'll call off your engagement. Now, pull over to the side of the road."

Skip maneuvered onto the shoulder of the road and stopped the van.

"Take off your glasses, and hand me your keys."

Shaughnessy laid his glasses on the passenger's seat beside him before handing his keys back to Rusty.

Rusty snatched the keys from his hand. "Now, get out of the van, nice and slow. Keep your hands where I can see them, and don't turn around."

Without a hint of resistance, the lad did as he was told. The pouring rain instantly drenched him.

Pocketing the keys, Rusty slid from the van and shut the door. "Hands on your head."

Like a soldier taken prisoner, the boy compliantly put his hands on his head, interlacing his fingers.

Despite the heavy rainstorm, Rusty grinned. *I guess the kid is too scared to put up a fight. This will be incredibly easy.*

Rusty pulled a bootlace from his trouser pocket and tucked the handgun under his belt. With confidence, he grabbed the lad's left wrist. Skip twisted free and spun around, kicking him in the stomach. Rusty sprawled to the muddy ground, gasping for breath. Lightning illuminated the entire sky, followed by a deafening clash of thunder, and the boy yanked out a gun. A gun? A kid his age packs a gun?

With adrenaline pumping through his system, Skip grabbed his gun, but the moment he drew it, someone tackled him from the side.

Where'd he come from?

Skip crashed to the ground and got hammered by the weight of the man who tumbled onto him.

"Wayne, he's got a gun!" yelled the man lying on top of him.

An instant later, Skip felt the weight of a second man as the two of them wrestled him for his gun and wrenched it from his grasp. Yanked to his feet, Skip struggled against the men who shoved him onto his stomach over the hood of his vehicle. They jerked his arms behind his back and securely bound his wrists together before yanking his cap down over his eyes.

"I'm glad you guys made it. I was losing the fight," said Rusty.

"We almost lost you in this storm. It's hard to see tonight. You got the keys to his van?"

"Yeah."

"Good. Take it up the road to the all night mini market and park it. We'll be right there to pick you up."

Grasping Skip's arms, the two men dragged him down a slippery slope.

"No," cried Skip. *"Let me go."* He struggled to break free, resisting with every ounce of strength he could muster. Unable to see where he was going, he slipped and tripped through a foot of water.

"This is good. No one driving by will see him from here."

They shoved Skip, and he sat down with a splash. The cold water washed over him. One guy strapped his legs together, and the other slapped masking tape over his mouth.

"Enjoy the night, kid. And for your own health, stay away from Cassandra McKenzie. One way or another, we intend to separate you two *permanently.*"

The men left him.

Sitting in waist-deep water, Skip shivered. The heavy downpour pounded him, and the ravine was filling up fast with rainwater.

Chapter 8

Taking Action

Cassandra paced back and forth in front of the telephone.

"Relax, Cassandra. He'll call when he gets home."

"Mom, he left thirty minutes ago. He should be home by now."

"The storm outside is pretty bad, so he'll have to drive a lot slower. Give him another ten minutes to call you."

Cassandra watched the clock's minute hand creep by, listening for the phone to ring. The instant the second hand rounded the twelve, ten long minutes later, she snatched up the receiver and dialed his number.

"Hello?"

Cassandra's heart sank at the sound of Erin's weary voice. "Mrs. Shaughnessy, this is Cassandra. Is Skip home, yet?"

"No, dear, and I wish he'd get home. I want to go to bed."

"He left here at nine thirty. I'm worried that something's happened to him."

"We'll give him another few minutes before calling the station. He may have stopped someplace on the way home."

"Not tonight. I assure you, he was heading straight home."

Erin slowly hung up the phone and peeked out the front window, hoping to see her mint green minivan pulling into the driveway. With a sigh, she dropped to her knees and prayed for Skip. When he wasn't home by ten fifteen, she called the police station.

"I'll alert second shift to watch for him," said Sergeant Kevin McAllister.

"*What.* You're not going out to look for him?"

"I'm sorry, Mrs. Shaughnessy, you called during the shift change, and with this severe weather, we're having more emergency calls than we can cope with. We can't spare anyone right now to go looking for Skip who's off-duty and only fifteen minutes late getting home."

"Kevin, something's happened to him."

"Give him a few more minutes. Maybe he stopped to lend assistance at the scene of a traffic accident."

"I suppose that's possible." But something told her that he didn't. Erin disconnected the call. Snatching the phone up again, she dialed Johnny's number.

Someone picked up the receiver, and she heard a loud noise on the other end. A moment later, a sleepy male voice came on the line. "Sorry. I dropped the phone."

"Oh, Johnny, did I wake you up? I'm so sorry. But I'm worried about Skip. He should have been home by now."

"He's out in that storm?" cried Johnny.

Erin could tell by the intensity in his voice that he was now wide awake and probably sitting up.

"I called the station, but Kevin said they don't have time to go looking for him. With this storm, they're dealing with a ton of calls."

"How late is he?"

"Well, he left Cassandra's house at 9:30 heading home. But he never got here."

Johnny heaved a sigh of relief. "That would make him only 20 minutes late, and with this storm, anything could have happened to delay him. But I'll get dressed and go see if he could be stranded on the road between your house and Cassandra's. Hopefully he didn't have an accident and is off the road somewhere."

"Thanks, Johnny." Erin slowly hung up the phone. She paced the floor, watching for her van and listening for the telephone.

Sitting in a foot of water, Skip shivered from the cold wind that pelted heavy rain against him. Thunder crashed overhead, and he jumped. Listening to the sound of the traffic on the road right above the ditch, he began to pray.

Lord, the thunder and lightning are a constant reminder of Your power and how You've promised to never forsake me. I trust You to direct Your mighty lightning bolts away from me and the water that surrounds me. Please protect me and send help because You're the only one who knows where I am.

Skip sneezed. He was already feeling sick. Trembling, he remembered last week's scripture memory verse from Sunday school.

God is our refuge and strength, a very present help in trouble.

In trouble, thought Skip. *God is a very present help in trouble.*

As the fierce rains continued to bombard the earth, the water he was sitting in was gradually getting deeper. By eleven o'clock, Skip had been in the ditch of water for an hour. If it didn't stop raining soon, he would drown.

Erin called the police station again at eleven o'clock.

"He's still not home?" asked Kevin.

"No. Now will you stop taking this so lightly and get someone out there to help Johnny find him? I'm worried sick."

"Johnny? Erin, he's on first shift. He's probably home in bed."

"No, he's not. I called him, and he went out in this storm to see if he could find Skip."

"Well, I see he didn't find him, because he just walked into the station. Okay, Erin, I'll send over an officer as soon as someone's available. If he should get home before then, call me."

Erin sighed. "Thanks, Kevin."

Lieutenant Johnny Marshall was dressed comfortably in jeans and a jacket since he was off duty. Six minutes before midnight, he spun a police cruiser into Erin's driveway.

Skip was reliable, prompt, and considerate. Since Erin had a tendency to worry about him, he always kept her informed of his whereabouts, plans, and intentions. So where was he, and why hadn't he called his mom?

Johnny wanted to wait for the rain to slow down before he exited his car, but every minute he delayed meant another minute that his best friend was out in that storm, possibly injured. Not willing to risk a delay, he and uniformed Officer Pete Kalen, dashed through the pouring rain to the Shaughnessys' front door. Almost immediately, the door swung open, and they hastened into the house out of the storm. Erin told them what little she knew. Then she handed Johnny the phone to call Cassandra.

"Do you know the route he took going home?" Johnny asked Cassandra. "Cause I've already made a quick run between your house and his, and I didn't see him."

"No, but Friday after he dropped me off, he took Kendola Road home. When he ended up in the ditch, he walked back to the bar to use their phone."

"How'd he end up in the ditch?"

"Some guy ran him off the road."

"Okay, well I'll drive back out to your house and see if we spot him along the way."

Johnny and Pete left. They drove slowly, watching for any stalled vehicles or other possible signs of trouble along the highway. The rain had slowed to a steady drizzle, and it was going on one o'clock in the morning by the time they reached Cassandra's house.

"No sign of him?" asked Cassandra.

Johnny shook his head. "Do you know any other routes that he takes to go home?"

"No. I know there are others, but I believe he favors that one because it's the most direct with the least amount of stops and turns."

"Okay, Cassandra. If you hear from him or think of something that you didn't already tell us, call the station."

"I will," said Cassandra.

Johnny and Pete hurried back to their cruiser. Johnny headed back toward Skip's house.

"Now what?" asked Pete.

"Back to his house by the most likely route he took."

"But we already checked it."

"So we check it again. We might have missed something."

While Johnny drove slowly toward Skip's house, Pete examined everything they passed, looking for signs of trouble or intrusion. When they reached the bar, they stopped long enough to look over the parked cars.

"Skip's car isn't here. Let's keep going," said Pete.

Johnny and Pete coasted up and down Kendola Road, finally pulling into the mini market a little before two.

"I think that's Erin's van," said Johnny. "Run a check on the tag while I go talk to the man inside the store." Hastening inside, Johnny cornered the man that worked there.

"I'm looking for the owner of that van," he said. "A young man about six feet tall, medium build, blond hair, wearing dark glasses. Was he in here tonight?"

"No. I haven't seen anyone matching that description."

"Hey, Johnny. That's Skip's vehicle, all right," called Pete, trotting through the door. "I found his keys and his gun in the glove box."

"Did you see who was driving that vehicle?" asked Johnny.

"Yeah. It's aggravating, too. A man drove up and parked that van in my lot. He didn't come into the store. He stood out in the pouring rain and climbed into a beige sedan with two other guys. Then they took off."

"Can you describe him?" asked Johnny.

"I didn't get a good look at any of them, but the man that drove the van was medium build, average height, and dark brown hair."

"What was he wearing?"

"A dark raincoat."

"Can you describe the other two?"

The man shook his head. "I only caught a glimpse of them in the car's dome light. I think they both had dark hair."

"Last question. From which direction did they come?"

The man pointed in the direction from which they had just come.

"Come on, Pete. That boy's in trouble."

Chapter 9

The Worry Warriors

Numb from the chilly water that had risen to his chest, Skip shivered uncontrollably. And it was still raining. Although the wind had died down considerably, it felt like the temperature had dipped into the fifties. The only thing keeping his teeth from chattering was the tape over his mouth. To add to his discomfort, he now felt sick to his stomach with a throbbing headache, and so congested, he could hardly breathe.

Lord, I know by now someone's out here looking for me, but if You don't guide the search, I'll either drown or suffocate before anyone finds me. And I'm so cold, I'm hypothermic.

Skip started coughing, but the tape covering his mouth made him choke. After nearly a full minute, he caught his breath.

And, Lord, if it's not too much to ask, please hurry. I'm freezing.

Johnny and Pete raced from the gas station and scrambled into the patrol car, heading back to Cassandra's house. Johnny's watch read two thirty as they drove up and down the road searching for any clues to Skip's whereabouts.

The police cruiser coasted along at ten miles an hour, illuminating the ground beside the road with the car's spotlight. Slamming on his brakes, Johnny pointed off to the side.

"Look, Pete." He leaped from the car and squatted close to the ground.

"Tire tracks," said Pete.

"Yes, but look at the angle. There were two cars parked here. One pointing straight ahead and one at a forty five degree angle."

Pete stood up and shined his flashlight on the ground in front of him.

"Look at the grass, Johnny. It's all trampled and muddy in this spot." Pete strolled along the road, examining the grass.

Johnny cupped his hands to his mouth and called out into the night. "Skip? Skiiiipp!"

Johnny carefully stepped to the edge of the ravine, calling Skip's name and shining his flashlight. "I can't see anything." He strolled along the edge of the ravine. "It's just too dark."

Skip's heart raced at the sound of his name. He desperately wanted to yell, but only muffled sounds escaped through his taped lips. He tried to get their attention by splashing in the water, but it was too deep.

"What should we do? Wait until daylight?" asked Pete.

No. No. Please, Johnny. I won't make it that long.

"Skip!" called Pete.

Johnny shrugged. "I don't know. I don't want to leave if he's out here. But I don't cherish the thought of traipsing through that water-filled ravine in the dark looking for him when we don't even know if he's here."

"Yeah, I hear you there."

Please, Lord Jesus, don't let them leave, pleaded Skip. *Show them where I am.*

Skip started coughing again. He gagged and choked, unable to catch his breath with the tape over his mouth.

"Pete, do you hear something?" Two flashlight beams pierced the darkness and shined around.

Struggling desperately to get their attention, Skip slipped and made a splash as he fell over in the water. Still choking, he struggled to get his head above water, but the water was too deep, and as he attempted to reposition himself, he lost his balance and plunged under again.

A Way to Escape

A strong hand grabbed his arm and pulled him above water. Still coughing and shivering violently, Skip felt the tape tanked off his mouth, and he gasped for breath. With the sound of a splash, Pete and Johnny lifted him into their arms and hoisted him from the water, setting him on the rain-soaked grass.

Johnny sliced the wet bootlace that bound his wrists and unstrapped his legs.

Pete wrapped him in a blanket that he retrieved from the patrol car. "I'll call an ambulance."

Skip removed his soaking wet ball cap. "P-p-p-please just t-t-t-take m-me home." His teeth chattered so badly, he almost couldn't talk.

"What happened, kid? Who did this to you?"

Skip shook his head. "I ... I ... I d-d-d-don't know."

"How did you get this bruise?" Johnny scooped Skip's wet hair aside to examine his forehead.

"I f-fell in the b-b-basement."

Pete and Johnny lifted Skip to his feet. Dizziness washed over him, and he swayed.

Johnny grasped his arm to steady him. "Kid, we're taking you to the hospital."

"J-J-Johnny, p-p-please t-t-take me home. All I need is d-d-dry c-clothes, a meal, and s-s-sleep. If you take me to the hospital, it will only keep me w-w-wet, hungry, and tired that much longer. So please take me home."

Supporting Skip on either side, the officers helped him to the cruiser. Overcome by another dizzy spell, Skip leaned against the car to steady himself.

Johnny opened the back door of the patrol car and motioned for him to get in. "You make a good case. Have you ever considered being a lawyer?"

"No." Skip crawled onto the hard plastic seat in the cage of the cruiser, unable to stop shivering.

Pete and Johnny jumped into the car and they took off. Skip rested his head against the seat, and his eyes dropped shut. He heard the Plexiglas window separating the front seat from the cage slide open, and he thought Johnny said something.

The warmth from the heater seeped into the back seat through the small window. Still shivering, yet beyond the point of exhaustion, Skip started to drift off. He was barely aware that the car had stopped. He heard a door open, then close again, before they started moving once more.

"Skip."

"Huh?" Skip jumped.

"Who did that to you?" demanded Johnny.

Without opening his eyes, Skip shook his head. "I don't know, but Linda's brother, Rusty, was involved."

"Linda who? What's their last name?"

"I don't know. She's a friend of Cassandra's. Including Rusty, I think there were three men. They told me to stay away from Cassandra. They intend to separate us one way or another."

"Can you describe them?"

"Only Rusty, because I got a good look at him when I was at Linda's house yesterday. As far as the other two goes, it was dark and everything happened so fast. They pulled my cap down over my eyes before I hardly got a glimpse of them."

"And their motive is to separate you and Cassandra?" said Johnny.

"Permanently. I'm afraid of what they might do to accomplish it."

Johnny pulled into Skip's driveway behind another car and cut the ignition. A moment later, the back door to the police car opened for him.

As Skip stepped from the patrol car, he noticed the McKenzies' car parked in his driveway. Just the sight of it made him lightheaded, and his knees felt weak. The last thing he wanted right now was sympathy, but between his mother and girlfriend, he knew it was unavoidable.

Softly closing the car door, Skip traipsed up the walk. The front door opened before he reached it, and he cringed.

Here it comes.

Bounding to his side, Erin and Cassandra both embraced and kissed him simultaneously.

Erin cupped his face in her hands. "Oh, sweetheart, you're soaked. You feel like you're running a fever. What happened?"

Skip swallowed hard and glanced over at Cassandra. "I'd rather not talk about it right now."

Entering the house, he caught sight of Melanie asleep on the sofa before glancing at Anita. Relief flooded her worry-filled eyes. That look stopped him cold. They'd been worried sick about him. It was a good thing, too.

They notified the police, who sent Johnny and Pete looking for him. Otherwise, he might still be sitting in that ravine full of water, if he hadn't drowned by now.

Skip smiled at Anita before starting up the steps. Overcome by a wave of dizziness, he grasped the railing to steady himself.

Erin turned to Johnny just as Anita joined them outside. "I'm grateful that you located Skip and brought him home. He doesn't look real happy to see us. Did I sound another false alarm?"

Her van turned into the driveway and stopped beside the police cruiser. Johnny's partner stepped out, handing Skip's keys to her.

"No, Erin, you saved his life tonight. We found him tied up in a ravine full of water off of Kendola road. He almost drowned. Pete and I pulled him from the water."

The ladies gasped.

"According to Skip, his assailants ordered him to keep away from Cassandra."

"Why?" demanded Cassandra.

"Don't know," said Johnny. "Be careful, Cassie. The next time, they may go after you."

Feeling faint, Erin brought her hand to her head and wavered.

Johnny steadied her. "You all right?"

"Oh, Johnny, it sounds like we came close to losing him tonight."

"Very close. He's thoroughly exhausted, so I wouldn't press him about it right now. We don't know all he's been through. Let him eat and go to bed. Goodnight, all."

Pete and Johnny left.

"Erin, now that he's home safely, we'll be going," said Anita.

Tears streaming down her cheeks, Erin hugged her. "Thank you for coming."

"It's almost four o'clock, and you haven't been to bed yet," said Anita. "Your little ones will be getting up soon. Why don't I just leave Melanie here. She's been asleep for a couple of hours. By the time your girls get up, Melanie will be rested enough to watch them while you sleep. That way, everyone can get some sleep."

"Thank you, Anita. That's very thoughtful of you. I appreciate it."

"I want to stay," cried Cassandra.

"No, Cassandra. You're coming home with me."

"Why does Melanie get to stay and not me?"

"Cause Melanie's asleep, and you're not. Now, get in the car." Anita hugged Erin. "Don't worry about him. I'll see you tomorrow."

"It's not fair. *I'm* his fiancée," grumbled Cassandra as she stomped out the door ahead of her mother.

As soon as they'd left, Erin re-entered the house and dead-bolted the front door. Expecting her son to be hungry, she trotted into the kitchen to fix him a sandwich. A few minutes later, Skip entered the kitchen fresh from a hot shower and dressed in warm, flannel pajamas and robe. He quietly sat down at the table and folded his hands.

"I'm sorry, Mom. I didn't mean to be rude."

Erin set his plate on the table in front of him and grasped his hand. Skip was trembling. "I'm relieved that Johnny found you and brought you home safely." Erin cupped his face in her hands and kissed his cheek. "I love you dearly. Goodnight, sweetheart."

Skip sighed when his mother left. Bowing his head, he thanked the Lord for his food and warm pajamas before gobbling his sandwich and washing it down with a glass of milk. He was still hungry, but right now he wanted sleep. Trotting up the stairs, he went to bed, intending to talk to Cassandra about their future together later that day.

Chapter 10

Pondering Possibilities

Thoroughly exhausted herself, Erin dropped into bed. Silence settled over the house for what seemed like only moments. Her son's panicked voice rousted her from a sound sleep, and she jumped out of bed.

"Cassandra!" yelled Skip. "Cassandra!"

Erin flew down the hallway, joining the girls, as they raced into his bedroom. Stephanie, her eldest daughter, darted to her brother's bed.

"Skip, wake up." She shook him. "You're having a nightmare."

Skip bolted upright in bed, breathing hard and trembling. He looked up, and his color drained when he saw his weary mother standing in the doorway with Melanie.

"Melanie, please take the girls out," said Erin.

Ushering the girls into the hallway, Melanie quietly closed Skip's bedroom door.

Erin sat down beside her son. "Judging from the looks of this bed, I'd say you've been all over it."

She grasped his hand. It was unbelievably hot. Erin stroked his flush cheeks and placed the back of her hand against his forehead.

"You're burning up. Let me get your temperature and bring you some Tylenol."

She hurried from his room, returning a minute later with the thermometer, a bottle of Tylenol, and a cup of cold water. Skip had lain back on the bed and closed his eyes again. Unloading her hands on the nightstand, Erin sat down beside him and shook down the thermometer before sliding it into his mouth.

Except for shivering, Skip lay perfectly still. His mother straightened his blanket and covered him. A moment later, she checked the thermometer. It registered 104.2.

"Sit up, sweetheart."

Skip silently obeyed. Erin emptied two Tylenol tablets into his hand and handed him the cup of water. He downed the tablets, emptied the cup, and slowly lay down again, curling up on his side. His mother tucked the covers around him and kissed his flush cheek before leaving his room.

Melanie met her in the hall. "What happened?"

"He had a nightmare, but I don't know if it was caused by running a high fever or his ordeal last night."

With a yawn, Erin returned to bed, but after taking a three-hour snooze she was now wide awake. Shortly before lunch, Anita arrived to pick up Melanie, but when she saw how tired Erin looked, she decided to leave Cassandra.

Cassandra and Stephanie helped Erin prepare lunch for the younger girls. After putting the two little ones down for their naps, they washed dishes.

"Cassandra, would you wake Skip and give him some Tylenol?" said Erin. "He's feverish, and it's been a good five hours since he's had any."

Cassandra wiped off the counter top and sent Stephanie to play checkers with Sandy. "Sure."

Fetching the Tylenol and a glass of water, Cassandra slipped quietly into his room. She knelt on the floor beside the bed. Gazing into his handsome face, she caressed his flush cheek. Then she placed her hand on his forehead.

"Oh, my, are you hot. Skip?" Cassandra nudged him. "Wake up, and take some Tylenol. Skip?"

"Hm?"

"Wake up, Skip." Cassandra tugged on him. "Come on, sit up."

Skip slowly sat up, and Cassandra placed two tablets in his hand. He swallowed them with a sip of water.

"Drink it all, sweetie. Every drop."

Skip emptied the glass. Handing it back to her, he once again snuggled under the covers and curled up on his side. Sitting down beside him, Cassandra ran her fingers through his soft, blond hair. Since he was asleep and they were alone, she bent down and planted a tender kiss on his temple.

Cassandra smiled. She absolutely adored him. She'd set her sites on him a year before they'd even met, and no one was going to stop them from getting married. *No one.* She rose to her feet and ran her fingers through his hair one last time before leaving his room and closing the door.

Tiptoeing down the hallway, Cassandra peeked in on Skip's two little sisters. Suzi and Scooter were both sound asleep.

With the house peacefully quiet, Cassandra padded softly down the stairs and into the living room where Erin napped in the recliner. Aware that their mother was sleeping, Stephanie and Sandy played checkers quietly on the floor.

Thinking this might be a good time to bury herself in a book, Cassandra grabbed the novel that she'd brought with her. The moment she got comfortable on the sofa, there was an unexpected knock on the front door.

She bounded to the door and peered through the peephole. It was Skip's partner. With a sigh, she swung open the door and stepped outside on the front step, pulling the door shut behind her. Hopefully, the knock hadn't woke Erin.

"Hi, Jesse. Skip's asleep."

"That's okay. I dropped by to talk to you."

"Me? How did you know I was here?"

"Your mother told me. Cassandra, who do you know that would go to such lengths to separate you and Skip?"

Cassandra shrugged. "I have no idea, Jesse."

"Do you have any former boyfriends?"

"No. Skip is the only boy that I've ever been allowed to date."

"Does your father know about your engagement?"

Cassandra shook her head. "No. My mom and I both thought it best if he didn't know. I mean, it was Skip's testimony that sent him to prison."

"Yes, I'm familiar with the case. Well, Cassandra, if you think of anything at all, please call the station." Jesse left.

Slipping back into the house, Cassandra bolted the door. Leaning against the front door, she slid to the floor, her mind racing. Who did she know that would do such a thing to Skip? He almost lost his life.

No longer interested in her book, Cassandra pondered Jesse's question. Her dad threatened Skip in court. But he couldn't possibly know that his daughter was engaged to be married to the boy whose testimony convicted him. Could he?

Chapter 11

Ignoring the Warning

Sitting on his bed studying the newspaper crossword puzzle, Skip looked up when a soft knock rattled his door.

"Come in."

Cassandra pushed open his door and strolled into his room. "Hi, Skip. Feel any better?" Crossing to his bed, she felt his face for fever. "Your fever finally broke."

"I do feel better."

Cassandra sat down beside him on the bed. "I'm glad because I've been putting off this question until you were well enough to consider it."

"What question?"

"I wanted to ask you about setting a date."

Skip pursed his lips, and he broke eye contact.

"What's the matter? You having second thoughts?"

"Um, well ..." With a sigh, he looked at her. "Did Johnny tell you anything about the other night?"

"Yes, and I don't know who's trying to separate us, but I love you, and I believe with all my heart that Jesus will protect us."

"I fear for your safety, though, Cassie. What if they go after you next? I don't want anything to happen to you."

With a smile, she squeezed his hand. "I'll be fine. Now, let's set a date."

Skip's sober expression didn't change. "Did you have a date in mind?"

"I know it'll put us in a time crunch, but let's plan for June 17th."

Skip's eyes widened. "What? Two weeks from Saturday? That won't give us enough time to get ready."

"I promise we'll be ready. But I want to marry you before you decide to back out on me." With a grin, Cassandra strolled out of the room.

Great. At the rate I'm saving for her ring, I won't have the money for another two months, and she wants to push up our date by three months.

The next day, Skip drafted Jesse to go car shopping with him. Without a doubt, he and Cassandra would need their own vehicle. He couldn't always take his mom's van.

Skip pulled into the used car lot and hopped out of the van. "Boy, Jesse, I sure would love to have a truck."

"Get one." Sliding out of the car, Jesse followed him. "Trucks are over there."

Skip led the way to the small, economy cars. "I have to consider what Cassandra would like, too."

"Cassandra doesn't even know how to drive."

"She doesn't?"

Jesse shook his head. "Oh, my, Skip. You're not even married yet, and she's keeping secrets from you already. Or are you just too much in love to notice those little things?"

Skip shoved him. "Mind your manners or go wait in the car."

Jesse saluted him. "Yes, sir."

While Skip and Jesse discussed the merits of a truck, they wandered through the lot.

A salesman joined them. "May I help you gentlemen?"

Skip and Jesse spoke simultaneously.

"No," said Skip.

"Yes," said Jesse.

"Well, which is it? Yes or no? Which one of you gentlemen is interested in buying a car today?"

"He is," they said in unison, pointing at each other.

"Did you have anything particular in mind?"

"Something with four wheels, a motor, and a steering wheel," said Skip. "Those are very important."

Jesse choked back a laugh.

The salesman cleared his throat and tried not to look annoyed. "Of course. Everything we have has four wheels, a motor, and a steering wheel."

"Seats, too?" asked Skip with such a straight face that the salesman burst into laughter.

"Seats, too," he said. "Come on. I'll make some suggestions based on the best deals in the lot."

Skip grinned at his partner, and they followed the salesman.

"I like this little Buick," said Skip. "But I'm not sure about the burgundy color. It's kind of loud."

"It's only a four seater," said Jesse. "Won't you need more room for your little sisters?"

Skip shook his head. "No. If I should have all the girls with me, then I'll take Mom's van."

"Will there be a trade in?" asked the salesman.

Skip shook his head.

While he and the salesman talked, Jesse wandered through the lot, looking over the other cars. "Hey, Skip, come here." The salesman followed as Skip hastened over to Jesse. "Did you see this metallic-blue Buick? It's the exact same kind, and it's cheaper."

Skip peered in the window. "It's only got 424 miles on it? How come this car is in the used car department? Was someone messing around with the odometer? That's illegal, ya know?"

The salesman shook his head. "No. The car is a '95. It was a demo, and the last person that test-drove it had a fender bender. So, rather than fix the dent, the sales manager opted to drop the price and move it to the used car department."

"Can we drive it? I like this one better. It's newer, got fewer miles. And I especially like the color."

"This one's a standard, Skip. The other one was an automatic," said Jesse.

"The other one costs almost three grand more."

Skip examined the dent and test-drove the vehicle. Then he went inside the dealership to dicker the price of the car. Skip and Jesse spent half their Saturday at the car dealership, but Skip drove his new car off the lot. Driving Erin's mint-green minivan, Jesse followed him to a friend's auto body repair shop.

"Hm." The Chinese man rubbed his chin as he examined the dent on Skip's new Buick. "Master Skip, this cost two hundred, seventy five dollar, but I give it you for one hundred and fifty, because you such good friend."

"Thanks, Mr. LuFong. When can you have it ready?"

"You pick up Tuesday afternoon. That soon enough?"

"That's fine." Skip left the car and scrambled into his mom's van beside Jesse. "And next week, after I get the car back, I'm going to have a police radio installed in it." Skip fastened his seat belt. "Home, James."

"Hey, I'm not your chauffeur."

Skip laughed.

The moment Skip entered the house, his mother handed him a stack of cards.

"Cassandra said for you to get these wedding invitations ready to mail."

"Uh, who do I send them to?"

"Here's a list of people and addresses."

Skip's mouth fell open. "All these people? I'll be addressing envelopes for two weeks."

"It's not that bad. Maybe Stephanie will help you. She has nice handwriting."

Skip and Stephanie sat down at the dining room table to prepare the invitations. Within an hour, they were finished.

"Hey, we ran out of addresses, but we have invitations left over," said Skip.

Stephanie laughed. "Skip, you have to buy enough invitations to make sure that everyone gets one. So sometimes you have extras."

Skip looked down at his little sister. "How did you get to be so smart?" Grabbing an extra invitation, he started filling it out, adding a personal message.

"Who's that one for?" asked Stephanie, leaning over to see what he was writing.

"This one's for the Masterson family. After all they did for me, I wanted to send them an invitation."

Withdrawing his wallet from his back trouser pocket, Skip pulled out a scrap of paper with their information on it. Billie, one of the Masterson triplets, had slipped it to him right before his family headed back to Forest Valley.

"What if they don't come?"

"Mr. Masterson has a multi-million dollar business to run, so they may not be able to make it. But if they don't get an invitation, they won't even know about it."

Skip signed his note, slid the invitation in the envelope, and addressed the envelope. Gathering together all the invitations, he stood.

"Hey, Scooter Pie. You want to walk to the mailbox with me and mail these?" Skip asked the youngest.

"I do," chorused Suzi and Sandy.

"Come on, then." Trailed by all four little girls, Skip strolled down to the mailbox.

As the day of the wedding drew nearer, Skip saw much less of Cassandra. Both were busy with the seemingly endless preparations. Skip picked up his new car from the body shop and found himself babysitting his sisters frequently while his mother helped Anita make wedding arrangements.

"Where are you taking Cassandra for your honeymoon?" asked his mother late Thursday evening.

Sitting at the dining room table studying the checkbook, Skip looked up. "Huh? What did you say, Mom?"

"What are you doing?" she asked him.

"Looking for more money, but I think it's hopeless. I had nine hundred dollars put aside. I paid a hundred and fifty to get the dent fixed on the car. That leaves me with only seven hundred and fifty dollars. And our rings will cost eleven hundred dollars."

"Well ..." Erin paused. "I have something for you, and I think now is the time to give it to you." His mother left the room. Returning a few minutes later, she handed him a sealed envelope.

"What's this?"

"Open it, Skip."

Carefully tearing the end of the envelope, Skip reached in and pulled out a stack of $100 savings bonds. His name was printed on each one.

"Wow," he gasped, slowly counting them. There were sixteen.

"I think your father would want you to have these now. He bought you one every year on your birthday. He intended to give them to you when you turned twenty-one. After he died, I couldn't afford to keep buying them."

"Thanks, Mom. Now I can afford to take Cassandra some place on our honeymoon."

The day before his wedding, Skip debated running away from home. He battled such a confusing mixture of emotions – all in connection with his wedding day. Excitement. Fear. Anxiety. Dread. How could one event elicit so many emotions?

Skip parked at the jewelry store and hustled inside. He and Cassandra had picked out these rings months ago and had been saving for them ever since.

The gray-haired sales clerk greeted him with a smile. "Ah, Officer Shaughnessy, let me get your rings. They came in this morning." He hurried to the back.

Skip had stopped in last week, putting in the order for the rings to be sized for their fingers and engraved with their names. The jewelry store normally required payment upfront before completing such an order, but the owner knew and trusted Skip, so she allowed him to pay for the rings by installments, making the first payment when he picked them up.

Returning with a package, the clerk handed it to Skip. Skip pulled out two small ring boxes and opened them.

"The set of rings is exquisite, an excellent choice," the sales clerk said. "Would you like to put this first payment on your charge?"

"Yes, sir." Skip handed the sales clerk his mother's credit card. When he and Cassandra returned from their honeymoon, he'd cash in those bonds to pay off everything he could.

The man smiled. "The lovely lady will be very pleased."

With a grin, Skip signed the charge slip. "Yes, sir, she will."

"So when is the big day?"

"Tomorrow."

Hurrying from the store, Skip placed the small package into the glove box and headed home. He'd see Jesse at the rehearsal dinner in a couple of hours, and he'd give him the rings at that time. After all, Jesse was his best man.

His ride home was quiet, and the road seemed deserted, but Skip spied a little red Focus in his rear view mirror. Rounding a blind curve, he braked to a sudden stop. A white pickup truck and a beat-up station wagon sat bumper to bumper, completely blocking the road. Both drivers stood near their vehicles, talking.

An accident? thought Skip. Because neither vehicle appeared damaged, he thought he'd check it out before calling it in on his recently installed police band radio.

Skip slid from his Buick and approached the two vehicles. He narrowed his eyes as he scrutinized the two drivers. He'd seen them both before.

The bar.

Hearing a car door slam behind him, he glanced over his shoulder.

Rusty.

He'd walked into a trap.

Chapter 12

Dropping a Clue

Skip slowly backed away, but they hurriedly surrounded him. These were the men who tied him up and abandoned him in a ravine full of water on a stormy night – the same men he saw in the bar. And it was certain that one of them had purposely run him off the road. And now he could identify all three of them.

"When's your wedding, kid?" asked the man to his immediate left.

Skip swallowed hard and glanced from one man to another. Rusty stood in front of his car door, so he couldn't escape by way of his vehicle. All he needed was a minor distraction and he could go for his gun, but the other man pulled his first.

"Don't be difficult. We'll find out one way or another. Now when and where is your wedding?"

Skip glared at them, but remained silent.

Angered by his defiance, the bartender grabbed his shirt and shook him. "You talk before I clobber you."

The man with the gun seized his wrist. "Knock it off, Wayne. You're not laying a hand on him."

"But, Sam ..."

"No buts, now frisk him. Last time, he had a gun."

Wayne shoved Skip over the hood of his car and frisked him, relieving him of his sidearm.

"Another gun," gasped Sam. "What kind of a hoodlum are you?"

Wayne and Rusty emptied Skip's pockets and searched his wallet for any information on his wedding.

"Sam, he's got a police shield in his wallet. He's a cop," exclaimed Rusty.

"A cop? That explains why he always carries a gun."

"Wow, look at all this dough." gasped Wayne.

Sam's mouth dropped open and he snatched a wad of cash from Wayne. "Holy mackerel. There must be over $500 here."

Replacing the money, Sam folded Skip's wallet and slid it into his own back pocket. With his gun, he motioned for Skip to move. "Kid, get in your car."

Quietly, Skip slid behind the wheel, and Sam climbed into the passenger's seat beside him. With the gun pointed at him and Sam's finger on the trigger, Skip sat perfectly still. He didn't want to jar or startle Sam into accidentally pulling the trigger.

Sam handed his truck keys to Rusty. "Follow us in my truck, and tell Wayne we'll meet him back at camp."

Rusty took the truck keys. After relaying Sam's message to Wayne, he moved his Ford Focus to the side of the road and jumped into Sam's truck.

Sam motioned with his gun for Skip to go. "Let's go, kid. We're going to stop by your house to drop off your car. Incidentally, I saw your driver's license, so I know where you live. You won't do yourself any favors by trying to go anyplace else. Understand?"

This guy was a step ahead of him. That's exactly what he planned to do. "Yes, sir."

Starting his car, Skip pulled behind Wayne's station wagon, and Rusty followed him in Sam's truck. But at the corner, Wayne turned left, and Skip turned right.

Sam laughed. "When we get to your house, park your car and quietly get into the back seat of my truck."

"Yes, sir." Skip glanced into his rear view mirror and over at Sam. He didn't dare accelerate suddenly or slam on the brakes. Sam's finger was still on the trigger, and the gun was aimed right at him.

"Sam, you don't want to do this. What do you hope to gain by keeping me from marrying Cassandra?"

"Shut up and drive."

"Did someone hire you?"

Sam ignored him.

Well, it was worth a try, thought Skip.

He turned onto his street, hoping none of his little sisters were playing out in the yard this afternoon. That could endanger them.

Reaching his house, Skip turned into the driveway and threw the car in park. Stepping from his Buick, he tossed the keys onto the front seat, hoping his mother picked up the clue, and he shut the car door. Skip and Sam both climbed into the back seat of the pickup, and Rusty took off.

"Look, kid," began Sam. "We're not letting you marry Cassandra. So we're holding onto you until after the wedding, and she'll think you stood her up. Now, when's your wedding, so we'll know when we can release you."

Skip remained silent. He watched the way as they drove him miles from home and finally stopped the car at a three-tent campsite on the outskirts of Medicine Bow. When their vehicle pulled in, Wayne stepped out of his tent to join them.

"Where's the rope?" asked Sam.

"Oh, yeah." Wayne ducked back inside his tent and emerged with rope in his hands.

Sam and Rusty both slid out of the truck, but Skip sat there, pondering his best means of escape.

Just then, Sam's car phone rang. Reaching into the front seat, he grabbed the receiver. "Yeah?" There was a short pause. With a grin, he looked at Skip. "Thanks, Kyle. We'll hold him until noon tomorrow. Bye."

Sam disconnected the call and reached over the front seat, holding out the receiver.

"What's your number? You're calling home. Tell your mom that you're out with some friends tonight and not to worry about you. You'll be home in the morning."

Reluctantly, Skip grasped the receiver and softly recited his seven-digit phone number.

The gun still aimed in Skip's direction, Sam punched in the numbers. "And watch what you say. I'd rather you not get hurt, but my friends don't think like I do. That's why they tied you up and dumped you in a ravine full of water during a thunderstorm. But if this loaded gun accidentally discharges while it's pointed at you, the results could be hazardous to your health."

Skip held the phone to his ear, listening to it ring. On the third ring, his little sister picked it up.

"Hello?"

His voice quivered as he spoke into the receiver. "Stephanie, get Mom please."

"Skip, where are you? It's time to leave for the rehearsal dinner."

"I know, Princess. Just go get Mom. Okay?"

Skip waited. Praying ... asking God for wisdom and guidance ... determined to fight.

A moment later, his mother answered the phone. "Skip, where are you? You brought the car home and took off again without it?"

"Um, yeah, I'm with Jesse."

"You left your keys on the front seat," said Erin. "Skip, is everything all right? I know you're not with Jesse, because Jesse just called here looking for you."

"Not to worry, Mom. Everything's fine. I'm going out with Jesse and some of the guys tonight. I wanted to celebrate my last night as a bachelor, so we're going out for some archery with the best doctor in the entire state of Wyoming. And I'll be out all night with Jesse, like usual."

Erin paused. "Um ... okay."

"Bye, Mom. Lord willing, I'll see you tomorrow." Skip hung up the phone and handed it back to Sam.

"That was a great job of lying you did, sonny. You're making our job easy." Sam replaced the receiver on his car phone and walked away. "Fellows, his wedding is at the Forest Valley Baptist Church tomorrow at eleven. Only the groom isn't going to be there. Tie him up." Sam stepped into a tent.

Skip looked from side to side as the rear truck doors were both opened. This might be his only opportunity to escape. Wayne stood at one door, while Rusty stood at the other. Although Rusty held the rope, Skip had already tussled with him once and knew that he wasn't a very good fighter.

Moving quickly, Skip scrambled toward Rusty and jumped from the vehicle. Rusty grabbed his arm. Skip twisted free and spun a round kick into the back of his legs. Rusty's legs buckled, and he collapsed. As Wayne raced around Sam's super cab pickup to help his friend, Skip spun around and threw a hard side thrust kick into his stomach, knocking the wind out of him. Leaving two of his abductors momentarily incapacitated, he bolted before the other one returned.

Chapter 13

Enlisting Help

Emerging from the tent, Sam glanced around and saw no one. The vehicle was there with both rear doors thrown open wide, but where were Skip and his partners?

"Rusty? Wayne?"

He heard groaning coming from the other side of his truck. Sam hustled around his vehicle and grasped Rusty's arm, helping him to his feet, while Wayne lay on the ground gasping for breath.

"What happened? Where's the kid?"

"He got away," said Rusty, rubbing his leg. "Boy, is he strong. He kicked me so hard, I thought he broke my leg."

"Oh, great. This is my fault. He'd been so co-operative up until this point, I let down my guard. I should have been out here helping you guys with him."

Wayne struggled to his feet still gasping for breath. "What ... what are w-w-we going to do?"

"We have to find him," said Sam. "Did either of you guys see which direction he ran?"

Rusty and Wayne both shook their heads.

"He probably headed back to the main road," said Sam. "Wayne and I will take the truck and see if we can spot him along the road. You see if you can track him down on foot."

Rusty threw up his hands and stumbled backward. "Not me. I've had encounters with him twice now, and I've lost both times. I think I'll head home. Right now Kyle needs me more than you guys do."

"Well, it's imperative we find him. For a hundred grand, we have to keep him from marrying Cassandra McKenzie, and if you leave now, that'll reflect on your cut."

"You think? You're getting paid through Kyle, and I'll be with him already when he gets the money. So I'll get my share before you see a dime of it. Here are your truck keys."

Rusty jumped into Wayne's station wagon and turned the key which was already in the ignition.

"I'm borrowing your car, Wayne, since mine is back in Forest Valley on the side of the road. I'll leave your car there and your keys under the rear floor mat."

Without waiting for a response, he drove away.

"Well, how do you like that?" gasped Wayne. "He didn't even ask."

Sam glared after Rusty before turning to Wayne. "You okay?"

Wayne looked a little peaked. Drawing in a deep breath, he nodded.

"Well, it's just you and me now. Jump in the truck, and let's go find that boy. After all, you owe him a kick in the stomach."

Skip raced through the woods toward the highway. He dodged trees and leaped over logs like he was running an obstacle course. He never looked back. It was almost five miles to the road, and he ran the entire distance. Just as he reached the edge of the woods, Sam's pickup whooshed by. Skip ducked behind a large tree to keep from being spotted.

Sam followed a bumpy dirt road to the main highway and turned right. A couple of miles down the road, they spotted a little ranch-style house right off the roadway.

"Sam, maybe we should stop there and ask if they've seen him."

Sam grinned. "Wayne, that gives me an idea." He smacked the brakes and turned sharply into the driveway. "You be quiet, and let me do the talking."

The men slid out of the truck and hurried to the front door, banging loudly. Sam pulled Skip's wallet out of his hip pocket. A middle-aged man greeted them at the door.

"Can I help you gentlemen?"

"I hope so. My name is Sam Richter and this is Wayne Thomas. We're with the state police." Opening Skip's wallet, he flashed Skip's police shield before closing the wallet and re-pocketing it. "We're on the trail of a felon and want to alert you folks that he was seen in this area."

"Gracious, what does he look like?" asked the man's wife, joining her husband at the door.

"He's young, good looking, blond hair, dark glasses. He was wearing a short sleeve blue shirt and pleated, khaki dress slacks. He's desperately seeking a phone to notify his partner of his whereabouts. So if you should see him, don't open your door or let him in. Just call me at this number." Sam jotted down the number to his car phone and handed it to the man. "We'll come right away."

"Is he armed and dangerous?" asked the man.

"No. In fact, he's quite charming, so don't let him deceive you. He may even try to convince you that he's a police officer."

"Thanks for the warning, Officer. We'll call you if we see him."

"Great. Oh, would you do me a favor and call your surrounding neighbors and businesses to alert them also."

"We'd be glad to," said the man.

"Thanks much. And feel free to give them this number so they can contact me."

"We most certainly will. Thank you for stopping by."

From the wooded area across the street, Skip crouched low, watching as Wayne and Sam drove away.

"Lord, please help me. I'd imagine those two crooks just told a pack of lies about me, so I'm not sure what to expect, but I'll need help getting home."

The moment Sam's pickup truck disappeared from view, Skip emerged from hiding and crossed the street to the house.

Chapter 14

Deciphering the Clues

The instant her son disconnected his call, Erin furiously scribbled down everything he told her.

Archery? No way. Skip wasn't interested in anything but baseball.

To the best of her knowledge, he'd never even picked up a bow and arrow. And he *never* stayed out all night with Jesse. That meant only one thing – he was in trouble and trying to tell her something. But what? She had no idea how to interpret his clues. Snatching up the phone again, she called Johnny to inform him of Skip's plight.

"Did he tell you where he was calling from?"

"He told me that he and Jesse were going out for some archery with the best doctor in the entire state of Wyoming. He also said that he'd be out all night like usual whenever he was with Jesse."

"Hm. Well, let me think on this and see what I can come up with."

"Hurry, Johnny. His life might be in danger."

"Believe me, Erin, I will not rest until I know he's safe."

Skip trotted up to the house. Standing beside the door, he flattened himself against the side of the house before reaching over and rapping on the door. Moments later, the door opened. Seeing no one, the man opened it wider and stepped onto the porch step, glancing around. He jumped when he saw Skip.

"Please, sir, may I borrow your phone? It's an emergency. I'm a police officer from Forest Valley. I've been abducted and robbed. The men that stole my wallet have my police shield and may be masquerading as cops."

The man narrowed his eyes, studying Skip. "Hm. They said you were charming and may try to convince me that you're a police officer."

"I *am* a police officer. Please let me use your phone to call my station. And anyone there can verify that I work there."

The man scrutinized Skip. His skepticism was obvious. "All right, but make it snappy." He motioned for Skip to enter the house.

Both the man and his wife followed Skip, watching him closely. Skip dialed the number and waited.

"Forest Valley Police Department. Officer DeShea."

"Tim, this is Skip. I've been abducted and robbed. Right now there are two men after me, and I'm stranded on the outskirts of ..."

The phone went dead.

"Hello?" Skip looked around and jumped at the sight of a shotgun pointed in his direction.

"Get out. You're not meeting your partner around here."

Skip slowly retreated. "I was talking to the dispatcher of the Forest Valley Police Department."

"Sure you were. Now get out before I find a reason to pull the trigger."

Dashing out the door, Skip heaved a sigh of frustration. He hiked along the highway, heading north, hoping to catch a ride. If he had to walk the distance, it might take him two days to get home.

Johnny jumped into his car and raced to the police station. He found Captain Paul Kramer waiting for him.

"The briefing room, Johnny. Erin has already called and left us with a puzzle to unravel. In addition, Skip called a few minutes ago."

"He did? Where is he?"

"Don't know. Before he could tell Tim, the phone went dead. He said he's been abducted and robbed. There are two men after him, and he's stranded."

Johnny followed Paul into the briefing room where several other officers were waiting.

"Have a seat, Johnny, and help us decipher Skip's message."

"Captain, we've been studying this for several minutes," said Sergeant Kevin McAllister. "Big deal that Skip likes archery and shooting arrows with a doctor. What's that got to do with anything?"

"Absolutely nothing," spouted off Officer Craig Bradley.

"Get on patrol," order Kramer. "You don't even belong in this meeting."

With a frown, Craig left the room.

The wheels turning in his brain, Johnny responded to Kevin's question as if Craig had never even spoken. *"Everything,"* he exclaimed. "Skip has never shot an arrow in his life. He's not the least bit interested in archery."

"And what does he mean by 'the best doctor in the state of Wyoming'" asked Detective Rick Johnson. "Does Skip have a doctor friend we could call?"

"Not that I know of," said Johnny. "But he didn't make reference to a local doctor. He said 'the best doctor *in the entire state of Wyoming.'"*

"And what's that got to do with archery?" asked Kevin.

"Maybe nothing," said Johnny.

"Maybe everything," added Rick.

Captain Kramer slowly stood. "Well, gentlemen, let's look at the Wyoming state map. Skip said he was with the best doctor in the entire state of Wyoming. If we can figure out what part of the state he lives in, maybe we'll find Skip."

Johnny joined the other officers as they gathered around the map.

"Well, he can't be too far out," said Rick. "Because they would have taken him by car. So we need to look at some of the surrounding cities or regions like Casper or Alcova or Medicine Bow..."

"Medicine Bow," gasped Johnny.

"Best doctor in Wyoming," said Paul.

"Bow and arrow," added Johnny. "Archery. Skip's in or near Medicine Bow. Captain, may I have permission to go out there?"

"You and Pete clock in and go. You're on department time. No uniforms. Medicine Bow is out of our jurisdiction."

Skip hiked along the shoulder of the endless country road that ran parallel with the woods. He estimated he was nearly one hundred miles from home, stranded without a car, money, identification, or a jacket. He shivered and rubbed his arms. Night was falling, and so was the temperature.

Headlights practically blinded him, and the approaching vehicle swerved toward him. Recognizing the truck, Skip didn't wait to see the occupants. He bolted. Wayne leaped from the vehicle and raced after him. Sam spun the pickup about and accelerated, screeching to a halt in front of him. Changing direction, Skip darted into the woods and disappeared. His abductors abandoned their truck and raced after him on foot.

Skip darted through the dim forest for almost a mile, finally removing his dark glasses and sliding them into his shirt pocket. Confident he'd lost his pursuers, he sat down on a fallen log to catch his breath. Skip watched, anticipating the arrival of his abductors, but they never showed.

What wimps. They can't even run a mile.

Skip enjoyed a brief rest before traipsing back to Lincoln Highway. He was still a distance from Medicine Bow. Hiking in the shadows of the wooded area, he attempted to duck out of sight every time he saw headlights coming from either direction.

Unfortunately, his wooded cover grew thin. That meant he wasn't far from Medicine Bow. There would be people there that might be willing to help him, but he'd have no place to hide if Sam and Wayne were notified of his whereabouts.

Thirty minutes later, he spotted an open diner. With a weary sigh, he quietly entered, scanning the walls for a public telephone. Seeing none, Skip strolled over to the counter and sat down on a bar stool. The bright light made him squint, so he slipped his dark glasses back on.

"I'll be with you in a moment, sir," said the young waitress, hurrying into the kitchen.

Skip relaxed, waiting patiently for her return. Surely, she would let him use their telephone to call the police station.

Pushing open the swinging kitchen door, the girl returned with a bounce in her steps. "Okay, now what ..."

With one glance at him, her smile faded, and she stumbled backward.

"Ma'am, may I please borrow the phone to call the police? It's urgent."

A man stepped out of the kitchen with a rifle. "Not as urgent as your need to leave."

Skip ducked out the door before that man pulled the trigger. Hungry, cold, and tired, he shoved his hands into his pockets trying to generate a little warmth.

Now that's the second guy who's done that to me, Lord. He treated me like a criminal.

Skip glanced around for a place to duck out of sight. Right now, darkness was his friend, and he slipped into the shadows behind the building. If there was anything he was certain of, it's that Sam would show up looking for him.

A few minutes later, headlights pierced the darkness, and Sam's truck pulled into the parking lot. The truck doors slammed shut, and he heard voices.

"Did you see which way he went?" asked Sam.

"No, I didn't see him at all," said Wayne. "But he's around here somewhere. He's been walking and running for nearly two hours now. He's got to be tired."

"Well, he's not the only one."

A Way to Escape

How did they find me again? Skip crept behind the diner and ducked down behind a pile of empty boxes, leaving Wayne and Sam talking. *Wherever I stop to ask for help, people are coming after me with guns. This guy must have the whole county looking for me because as soon as I talk to someone, they run me down. I'm not asking anybody else for help. It's too risky.*

Chapter 15

The Empty Search

It took Pete and Johnny a good hour to reach Medicine Bow. They shot straight down Highway 487, watching for any pedestrians along the way.

"It's dark out. If Skip's around here, it will be difficult to spot him," said Johnny as they passed a diner on the outskirts of town. "But we'll watch for anyone on foot."

"Maybe we could stop at a couple places to see if anyone has seen him."

"Good idea."

Seeing no one on foot and having no idea where to even begin their search, Pete and Johnny randomly selected a small ranch-style house right off the roadway near a wooded area. With lights on in the house, they knew that the homeowners were still awake, so Johnny parked the car and they hurried to the door, pounding on it. A moment later, the door swung open, and a middle-aged man greeted them with a smile.

"How may I help you gentlemen?"

Johnny and Pete both opened their wallets and displayed their police shields.

"More police officers? Sorry fellows, I told those other two cops everything I know."

"Sir, I don't know what you're talking about," said Johnny. "We're looking for someone."

"So were they."

"Oh, really? Who were they looking for?" asked Johnny.

"Some felon."

"Well, we're looking for a fellow police officer," said Pete.

"We're from the Forest Valley Police Department." Johnny pulled a photo of Skip from his wallet and handed it to the man. "Here's a picture of him."

The man gasped when he saw the picture.

"I take it, you've seen him," said Johnny.

"This fellow is a police officer?" he asked weakly, handing the photo back to Johnny.

"Yes, and it's imperative we find him. There are some men after him, and his life is in danger."

"Oh, my. He was here, and so were the men after him. They told me they were state police officers. They showed me a badge and said they were tracking a felon. I believed them. They asked me to call friends and businesses nearby and alert them to be on the lookout for him."

"Did you do that?" asked Pete.

The man nodded. "Immediately. But that's not the worst of it. After this young fellow left here, I called these 'so called' cops and gave them his exact location."

"Which direction did he go?" asked Johnny.

"Toward Medicine Bow."

"Please, sir, call all the folks you talked to earlier and tell them that he is a police officer in trouble. Ask them to allow him access to a telephone." Johnny and Pete dashed back to their car.

"Right away." The man disappeared into the house.

Pete and Johnny followed Skip's direction. At least now they had a starting point. Watching for any pedestrians along the roadway, they passed the diner and a white pickup truck, parked on the shoulder of the road.

Johnny turned toward town. It was the safest place for Skip to be hiding, so it was the most likely place for them to find him. And the town was so small that he and Pete could probably do a drive-thru of the entire town in less than 30 minutes, just to see if they spotted him. Medicine Bow didn't even have a police department.

Once again, Sam and Wayne lost Skip. But then, they weren't really looking for him too hard. They were both exhausted. After a brief search, they returned to Sam's pickup.

"Look, Wayne, this is a total waste of time. We don't need him anyway."

"We don't? Then why are we looking for him?"

"We want to make sure he misses his wedding, and he probably will," said Sam. "He's stranded with no money or means of transportation. Plus, we have everyone around here thinking he's a felon, so no one will let him borrow a phone. Consequently, he has no choice but walk. And if he walks all night, he may get home by eleven tomorrow night."

"Does that mean our job is over?"

"Probably. However, to play it safe, let's head to Forest Valley. Around ten o'clock tomorrow morning, we'll stake out the church. If he *should* get there, we'll intercept him and keep him from going inside."

"Great plan. Only one problem. How are only two of us going to stop him? The first time, it took all three of us to get him down."

"Hm, good point," said Sam. "It did take the three of us, and we had the element of surprise on our side. Otherwise, he might have left us in that ditch of water."

"Well, I'm with Rusty. I'm not going up against him again, at least not without help."

"I'll get us some help. There are a couple guys who owe me favors. I'll cash in on those favors for tomorrow morning, on the outside chance he makes it there in time. Then we'll be prepared."

Skip crawled out from behind the boxes. Sam and Wayne didn't venture behind the store looking for him.

Glancing around, he saw the pickup was gone, which meant they were gone.

Cramming his cold hands into his pockets, he started walking. Lincoln Highway ran right into 487. Skip crossed the road, and started his lengthy northward hike along the smoothly paved shoulder. Eventually, it would lead him home. Periodically he saw car headlights heading one direction or the other, and he hoped it wasn't Sam, still looking for him.

Skip looked up at the star sprinkled sky as he walked. A nearly full moon illuminated his path. *Thank you, Lord, for that big night light in the sky.*

His glasses in his pocket, he shivered constantly, and he was nauseated from hunger. It was well past midnight and a car hadn't passed him from either direction in almost an hour.

Sitting in the parking lot of a closed service station, Johnny heaved an exaggerated sigh as he slowly hung up the pay phone.

"Well, Skip hasn't called the police station," he said, sliding behind the wheel of the cruiser. "Pete, where is that boy? We've been up and down every road in town a dozen times or more."

Pete dropped into the front passenger's seat next to Johnny. "I don't know, Johnny. We've banged on door after door. Except for that home owner and the cafe manager, no one else has seen him."

"He's in big trouble," said Johnny. "Skip is very resourceful. If there was a way for him to get to a phone to call the station, he would have done it by now. Pete, we had half the residents from Medicine Bow out here watching for him, ready and willing to assist him. He never came in contact with any of them. That only means one thing. He was forcibly stopped."

"Or he was afraid to ask anyone else for help," said Pete. "Don't forget, two people chased him out with guns, threatening to shoot him. He might have been afraid that the third person would pull the trigger."

Johnny heaved a sorrowful sigh and cranked up the car. "Point well taken." He turned out of the parking lot toward home. "Which means, he may be walking home. Let's head back to Forest Valley and see if we can spot him along the road."

"What if we don't?"

"Then I have an unpleasant but vital task waiting for me back in Forest Valley. I have to inform Cassandra that Skip may not make it to the wedding." Johnny's voice cracked.

"He's very special to you. Isn't he?"

"Skip's father was my partner and my very best friend. He was killed by a shotgun blast and died in my arms. The last thing he said to me before going to meet the Lord was, 'Johnny, Skip's headed for trouble. Help him like I helped you.' I promised Stephen that I would take care of Skip. Pete, I love that boy dearly. I'll die if anything happens to him."

Chapter 16

The Lord's Direction

Plodding along on the shoulder of the highway, his arms crossed in front of him, Skip rubbed them to generate warmth. A soft glow illuminated his path. He glanced behind him and saw that it was a semi tractor-trailer.

Oh, it's just a truck. Thank goodness for that.

The truck pulled onto the shoulder of the road and slowed to a stop right in front of him. Skip backed away from it.

The driver rolled down the passenger's window. "Hey, kid, you want a lift?"

Skip looked up at the man, reluctant to accept his offer. Could this be another of Sam's traps? Shivering, he rubbed his arms.

"Look, son. I don't make it a habit to stop for strangers. But you look cold, and you've got to be tired. The last town I passed was Medicine Bow. That was a good ten miles ago, and I haven't seen any stalled vehicles along the way, so you've walked at least ten miles. It's almost one a.m., about forty-five degrees out tonight, and you're not even wearing a jacket. And in case you don't know, it's twenty miles to the next town. Now I have a deadline, so if you want a ride, get in the truck."

The driver opened the door for Skip. Grasping the side bar, Skip climbed into the warm truck.

"Thanks. I appreciate you stopping for me. My name's Skip."

"Alex," said the trucker. Shifting gears, he accelerated once again. "So where are you headed?"

"Home."

"Where do you live?"

"Forest Valley."

"Good gracious. How did you get stranded so far from home?"

"It's a long story."

"I've got time," said Alex. "Why don't you share it?"

"Well, I'm supposed to get married this morning at eleven."

"And you got scared at the last minute so you ran away from home." Alex stated it like it was a fact.

Skip smiled. "No, someone else is trying to keep me from marrying the girl, so they abducted me and took me to the wooded area on the other side of Medicine Bow. I escaped, and they've been trying to catch me. That's why I was reluctant to accept your offer."

"You mean to say, you've walked all that way?"

"Yes, sir. And I'm awfully tired."

"When was the last time you've eaten?" asked Alex.

"Noon yesterday."

"Well, you must be famished. Here, have some fried chicken." Reaching between the seats, Alex opened his cooler and pulled out a sealed container full of chicken, handing it to Skip. "My wife always packs me a ton of food. Eat all the chicken you want. In fact, help yourself to anything else you want. I have bread, cole slaw cups, cookies, pudding, soda, water, chips, and lots of fruit."

"Thank you, sir. That's kind of you."

Alex smiled. "No problem, Skip. God has blessed me with so much that I'm delighted to share. I almost drove right by you, but I felt the Lord direct me to stop. So I did."

"I appreciate it," said Skip. "Where are you headed?"

"Billings, Montana, but I have to go right through Forest Valley."

"You do? That's great. I may be getting married after all."

Skip bowed his head and thanked God for his food. After he'd eaten and put away the food, he closed his eyes and dozed in the nice warm truck. He'd barely slept an hour when Alex roused him.

"We're in town, Skip. Where do you want dropped off?"

Yawning, Skip sat up and glanced around. "The police station is on the next corner. I can call home from there."

Alex maneuvered his big rig over to the curb.

Skip smiled. "Thanks for the lift, Alex. If you're ever in this area, stop by and see me. You can always contact me through the police department."

"I'll do that."

Skip jumped out of the truck and waved at Alex as the truck pulled away. With no keys, he couldn't get into the station, so he entered through the front door and rang the bell.

"Skip," cried Sergeant Kevin McAllister. He buzzed Skip in. "What happened? Where have you been? Where are Pete and Johnny?"

Pulling open the door, Skip entered the office and grabbed the phone.

Hearing the excitement, Officers Craig Bradley and Jerry Jordan hustled over to Skip.

"Pete and Johnny?" Skip paused. "I don't know."

"We deciphered your code, and Captain Kramer sent them to Medicine Bow searching for you."

"I didn't see them. I did a lot of hiding. I would have called the station, but no one would let me use their phone. The men that kidnapped me took my wallet. They have my driver's license, my police shield, and over five hundred dollars that belong to me." Skip dialed his home phone number.

"Get an APB. out on them immediately." Kevin sprinted down the hall. "I need to call the chief and the captain."

Craig and Jerry returned to writing their reports.

Listening to his phone ring, Skip waited for his mother to answer.

"Hello?"

"Hi, Mom, I'm calling from the station. I'll be here for awhile because I have to file a police report."

"All right, Skip. I'm so glad to know that you're safe. How are you getting home?"

"I'm sure one of the guys will bring me home. See you in a couple of hours."

As soon as Skip hung up the phone, he jotted down a thorough description of his abductors and handed it to the dispatcher, who promptly notified all patrol officers. Collecting the necessary paperwork, Skip slipped into the unoccupied break room to complete a report on the incident.

Johnny and Pete plodded into the station, heading straight for the break room.

"Well, it's about time you two got back," said Craig. "While you and Pete were playing hopscotch through Carbon County, we were back here doing all the work."

"All what work?" asked Pete.

Johnny narrowed his eyes. Craig and Jerry soberly looked at one another.

"Do you guys know something I don't?" asked Johnny.

Jerry looked down at the floor. "Um ... well ... It's about Skip. He's ..." His voice trailed off.

"He's what?" demanded Johnny.

Craig and Jerry exchanged glances and exploded into laughter.

"Never mind. It's better that you not know," said Craig.

Jerry nodded in agreement.

Johnny frowned. "It's better that I not know what?" If anything happened to Skip, he'd die, and these guys were making light of it.

Just then, Kevin strolled in. "Hey, you guys get back on the street. There's work to do." He chased the third shift officers out of the station. "Pete, clock out and go home. Johnny, would you do me a favor and run someone home?"

"I'm beat. Can I call him a cab?"

"He can't pay for it. He was robbed and has no money. In addition, he lives clear across town." Motioning for Johnny to follow him, Kevin led him into the break room. Skip looked up from his report.

At the sight of Skip, Johnny's heart missed a beat. He dodged around a table and a couple of chairs to reach him and pulled him into a hug. Releasing Skip, Johnny grasped his arms, held him at arm's length, and examined him for abuse. He didn't see one mark on him. "Kid, I am so glad to see you."

"Thanks, Johnny. For awhile I wasn't sure I'd make it back."

"Skip, Johnny will run you home," said Kevin.

"Yes, sir."

Skip sat down to finish his report.

By the time Johnny dropped him off at home, the sun was rising.

"What time are you supposed to be at the church?"

"Ten thirty."

"Then I'll be here by ten," said Johnny. "We're giving you a police escort."

Chapter 17

Baiting the Trap

Morning came too fast for Skip. He had barely showered and eaten by the time his family was up and moving. Skip dressed in a long-sleeve, pastel-blue dress shirt, shiny black trousers and suit jacket with a yellow tie. Those were the colors that Anita and his mother had picked out.

His mother's voice drifted from the bathroom down the hall. "Scooter, you come back here. Sandy, grab her for me."

Hearing his mother yell, Skip stepped into the hallway. Quick as a rattler, he snatched up three year old Scooter just as seven-year-old Sandy ran into him, chasing her naked little sister.

"Where do you think you're going?" Skip asked Scooter. "You can't go to my wedding with no clothes on. People will talk."

Erin started laughing.

Despite trembling hands, Skip helped his mother get his little sisters ready, dressing them in their fancy blue pastel dresses which matched his shirt. Then Erin fixed their hair with yellow ribbons the same color as his tie.

"Relax, sweetheart. I know you're nervous, but it will soon be over."

"Mom, does Cassandra know about yesterday?"

Erin shook her head. "No, dear. Johnny and I thought it best not to tell her unless we absolutely had to."

Around nine thirty, a three-car caravan pulled up in front of his house. Skip ushered Johnny, Jesse, and Kevin into the house, and they followed him into the kitchen. All dressed for the wedding, they matched Skip with the same black suit, blue shirt, and yellow tie.

Despite the fatigue in their eyes, revealing that they'd all shared a rough night, the four of them seated themselves around the table, discussing their strategy. Erin stood behind Skip's chair, her hands on his shoulders, listening to the conversation.

"Skip, how many are we dealing with?" asked Johnny.

"At least four. There were three men directly involved in my abduction. Linda's brother, Rusty, and two guys I saw in the bar. Their first names are Sam and Wayne. Then a man named Kyle called them with information on my wedding."

"Who's Linda?" asked Johnny.

"A friend of Cassandra's. I can't remember her address, but I can show you where she lives."

"Can you tell me where she lives so I can send a couple of officers out there right now?"

"I can do that." Skip sketched a map, labeling streets and marking the location of Linda's house, along with landmarks.

Johnny studied it before excusing himself to call the station.

"Why are they trying to keep you and Cassandra from getting married?" asked Kevin. "What are they hoping to gain?"

"I have no idea. They wouldn't tell me."

"Whoever it is must feel they have an awfully good reason," said Jesse. "They sound determined. I anticipate their next move is to stake out the church."

"My thoughts exactly," said Johnny, pulling out a chair and rejoining them. "We need to set a trap."

Erin gasped. "If you set a trap, you must have bait."

"That's right," said Johnny. "Skip's the bait."

Skip looked up at his mother. "Mom, those men abducted me at gunpoint and robbed me. How do we know they won't do it again? They must be caught."

"Are you willing to endanger your little sisters over this?"

"Heavens, no," said Johnny. "That's why Kevin's taking you and the girls to the church in his car. He will be with you at all times, and Skip will go alone."

Erin frowned. "I don't like the sound of that."

Rising to his feet, Johnny pushed in his chair. "Erin, he won't *really* be alone. We'll always be close by, but so our suspects will make a move, Skip will appear to be alone. And for your protection, Kevin will be with you and the girls."

"Only one problem," said Skip. "Sam stole my wallet, so I don't have my driver's license. To drive myself to the church, I'd have to drive illegally."

"We won't tell," said Kevin.

As the others rose from the table, Erin turned Skip around to face her, grasping his arms. "Do *you* want to do this?"

"I'm a cop, Mom. Yes, I do. They must be stopped."

Skip could tell that these arrangements did not please his mother. Regardless, she gathered together her little daughters and hustled them out the door to Kevin's car. Skip gave them a five-minute head start. Then he and the other officers followed them out the door.

Jesse climbed into his pickup and pulled away from the curb. Jumping into his car, Skip pulled out behind him, and Johnny's van brought up the rear.

Skip's mind raced – from the rehearsal dinner that he'd missed ... to his wedding ... to his kidnappers ... to his mother's concerns ... to the sting operation in the church parking lot right before his wedding.

His palms got sweaty, and his hands trembled. If anything went wrong, it could turn into a funeral. How could he explain to his mother how he got killed when she was so dead set against it, and they did it anyway.

That was certainly a lot to think about.

Sitting across the street from the church in Sam's super cab pickup truck, Sam and Wayne peered through binoculars, constantly scanning the parking lot and studying every vehicle that turned into the lot. Sam's friends, Chad and Erik, sat in a car on the far side of the church parking lot, observing activity and waiting to hear from Sam.

Sam keyed the mic to his two-way radio. "He ain't gonna make it. I suspect he's still walking."

"There's a lot of people arriving for a wedding that's been canceled due to the groom's disappearance," said Chad.

"They don't know that he's not gonna show. That's the beauty of it."

"You made him miss the rehearsal dinner last night. Don't you think they went looking for him?"

"I doubt they found him, but we'll hang tight a little longer."

"Sam." Wayne pointed at the metallic-blue Buick turning into the church parking lot.

Sam's eyes widened. "Never mind, Chad. He just pulled in."

"The little blue Buick?"

"That's him."

"Stay where you are," said Chad. "Erik and I will be right there."

Skip spun his Buick into a conveniently close parking spot while Jesse and Johnny drove around to the back lot. Glancing around uneasily, Skip sighed when his best friends disappeared from view. Now he felt alone – really alone – and vulnerable.

With an eerie feeling that Sam and his cronies were nearby watching him, Skip looked around again, hoping for the assurance that the police also had the area under surveillance, but he saw no evidence of their presence. That unnerved him.

Drawing in a deep breath, Skip collected all his courage and pulled his keys from the ignition. He looked over at the main entrance, wondering how quickly he could get from his car to the church entrance. Now he wished Johnny, Jesse, and Kevin had stayed with him. Undoubtedly, Kevin was in the church guarding his family, but where were Jesse and Johnny? He had to trust them to protect him. He couldn't panic and bolt toward the door.

Skip retrieved the rings from the glove box. He was every bit as nervous about his wedding as he was another possible abduction.

Here goes.

Pushing open his car door, he stepped from his vehicle. He dropped the two small ring boxes into his right trouser pocket. He glanced around and still saw no evidence of a police stakeout. With great restraint, he strode toward the church entrance. Six paces from his car, two vehicles suddenly stopped on either side of him.

Before he could run, Wayne and the driver of the other car grabbed him and threw him into the backseat of Sam's pickup truck. Skip tumbled into the passenger who was sitting behind the driver's seat, and Wayne scrambled in behind him.

Chapter 18

A Little Detour

Before Skip could assess his situation and formulate a quick plan of escape, the passenger he tumbled into snapped a handcuff bracelet on his left wrist and locked him to the extension bar on the driver's headrest.

With the squeal of tires, several unmarked cars screeched to a halt near the two vehicles, quickly boxing them in. Armed police officers jumped out.

Wayne yanked out a gun just as Officer Tim DeShea jerked open his truck door. Snatching the gun from his grasp, he seized the back of his shirt and dragged him from the truck. At the same time, Johnny pulled open Sam's door and jerked him out of the vehicle.

With a sigh of relief, Skip sat quietly in the back seat of the super cab pickup, watching his abductors forced to the pavement face down, searched, and handcuffed. Johnny located Skip's wallet in Sam's rear pocket.

And the church parking lot had become a crime scene a half hour before his wedding, involving not only him, but half the wedding party, including Jesse, Johnny, and Kevin.

As cars filed into the church lot and the time neared eleven o'clock, Skip knew he should get inside, but he didn't have his handcuff key on him. Uniformed officers took over, while those in the wedding dashed toward the church's main entrance.

"Greg, unlock these handcuffs," called Skip. *"Tim ... Sally ... anybody!"* Skip rattled the handcuff chain and attempted to jar the headrest loose so he could remove it, but it didn't budge. He watched the wedding party race toward the church entrance. "Somebody, unlock these cuffs." But there was so much commotion outside, nobody could hear him.

"Skip." Doing an immediate about face, Johnny raced back to the pickup and seized Skip's arm.

"Johnny, no. I'm handcuffed."

"You're what?" Johnny released him and patted his trouser pockets in search of his handcuff key. "Oh, man, I didn't bring my key. Why would I?"

Spinning around, he cornered the nearest officer. "Unlock Skip. He's handcuffed."

The instant, the handcuff bracelet slid open, Johnny seized Skip's arm and jerked him out of the truck. "Come on."

Skip raced Johnny into the church, falling in line behind the other officers as they filed down the side aisle of the church to the platform where Pastor Greene patiently waited for Skip.

Reaching into his trouser pocket, he pulled out the wedding rings and passed them to Jesse. Skip bounded onto the platform and grasped Pastor Greene's extended hand.

The pastor pulled him close. "Sorry you missed the rehearsal," he whispered. "But I'm glad you got here safely. Stand beside Jesse, watch Cassandra, and follow my lead." With a smile, the pastor released his hand.

From the rear of the auditorium, Kevin, Johnny, and Jesse stood on the right side of the platform facing the audience. Skip took his place next to Jesse, first in line. On the left side of the platform facing the audience stood Melanie, Stephanie, and Sandy, all wearing identical blue dresses with yellow ribbons in their hair.

A projector screen on the right side of the church displayed a continuous show of photographs of Skip, from infancy through high school. Whereas on the left side, there was a continuous show of Cassandra's childhood pictures. On the small table in front of them stood three white candlesticks in candlestick holders. The candlesticks on the right and the left were both lit, but the one in the center was not.

Erin and Scooter sat on the front row. Skip smiled nervously at his mom. As the piano started to play, little Suzi, now five years old, started down the center aisle carrying a small basket and tossing rose pedals from it as she walked. Reaching the platform, she stepped onto it and hurried to stand by her sisters.

As the wedding march sounded, the guests stood. Police Chief Cory Clark escorted Cassandra down the aisle.

Mesmerized by the sight of his beautiful bride strolling toward him in her flowing white wedding gown, his nervousness dissolved. When Cassandra finally reached him, Skip looked at Pastor Greene.

"Who gives this woman to be wed?" asked the pastor.

"Her mom," said Chief Clark with great pride in his voice. He grinned at Skip before joining his wife on the first row.

Now standing before Pastor Greene, preparing to exchange vows, Skip noticed that a third screen had just started displaying pictures of him and Cassandra together.

Jesse promptly passed him Cassandra's beautiful new ring. Skip fingered it, not certain when to place it on her finger until he glanced at Pastor Greene, who gave him a slight nod.

Facing Skip, Cassandra reached for his hands. Subtle, but easy to understand, Skip slipped the ring on her finger and took her soft hands in his, tenderly repeating the marriage vows after the minister.

Taking Skip's ring from Jesse, Cassandra slid it onto his finger, holding his hands and repeating the marriage vows. While they gazed at each other, the piano broke the silence, accompanied by a beautiful alto voice, and special music filled the auditorium.

Cassandra held his hands throughout the tender song that expressed the love they shared. Halfway through the last verse, Cassandra turned toward the candles, and Skip followed her lead. When she picked up the burning candle on her right, he picked up the burning candle on his left.

"Together," she whispered.

Together they lit the candle in the center. Then they each blew out their candle before returning it to the candlestick. Cassandra grasped Skip's hand tightly.

As the song concluded, Pastor Greene faced the audience. Quoting from the King James Bible, he said, "'And they twain shall be one flesh.' With great pleasure, I introduce to you Mr. and Mrs. Skip Shaughnessy."

Lifting Cassandra's silky white veil, Skip embraced her gently and planted his lips against hers. But when he released her, he and Cassandra both turned to face the audience, and Skip was stunned by the mixture of emotions emanating from the wedding guests.

The teenage girls were crying, as well as his family. His church family was clapping. His fellow officers were cheering. Everybody was standing. And as he scanned the crowd, he caught sight of Carl and Martha Masterson and their three beautiful teenage triplets, who were all waving.

With a big grin, Skip waved back. The instant he and Cassandra stepped off the platform, they were surrounded by people offering their congratulations. Shaking hands. Kissing the bride.

The church hosted their wedding reception in the fellowship hall.

The first thing Skip did was to catch up with Carl and Martha Masterson. They were now faithfully attending the Bible study with their three daughters, Billie, JJ, and Crystal. Martha had accepted Jesus as her Savior. Billie and JJ were doing some serious dating. And Crystal was thinking of going on the mission field with Michael, who was now her best friend. In addition, Michael managed to connect with his older sister, Mistie, and her family. *And what a reunion that was.*

Martha hugged Skip. "We will never forget you. We have to go. We have a long drive home. But we were not about to ignore that thoughtful invitation you sent us. You've not only changed the very direction of our lives, you changed our entire destinies. Thank you." She kissed his cheek.

Carl shook his hand. "Keep in touch. You know where we live. You are always welcome to stop by."

One by one, the girls hugged and kissed him.

"Send us pictures," said Billie. "We will always think of you like our brother."

The girls waved and followed their parents out the door.

Cassandra grabbed a quick bite to eat before she and Skip cut the cake. That's what she really wanted anyway. And this was a special occasion, so it was okay to eat two pieces.

Munching on her cake, Cassandra strolled through the huge, colorfully decorated room visiting with friends and family.

"Hey, Cassandra," called Jesse. "Congratulations for finally getting him to the altar."

Cassandra raised an eyebrow. "What do you mean? He was the one who proposed."

"No, no. I was referring to yesterday."

"What happened yesterday?"

"Oops, I think I wasn't supposed to say anything. Never mind, Cassandra." Jesse quickly disappeared.

"Hm." Cassandra glanced around for Skip. *There he is.*

Skip held his hand up to watch his ring glisten in the sunlight. Slipping up behind him, Cassandra looped her arm through his and snuggled up to him.

"I'm glad you made it to the wedding," she said. "It wouldn't have been the same without you."

Skip chuckled. "That's for sure."

"What happened yesterday?"

Skip slid his arm around her, and they started walking. "Well, it's kind of a long story, but to make it short ..." Skip gave a brief account.

Cassandra gazed up into his bright blue eyes. "You went through a lot to get back in time for our wedding."

"I love you, Cassie. I don't want anything to come between us."

"Skip, you're an angel." She squeezed his hand. "You're my angel." Reaching up, she gently kissed him. "I know I should have asked you this sooner, but I was so busy with our wedding arrangements that it slipped my mind. Were you able to get some time off for our honeymoon?"

"I'm still on administrative leave until I hear otherwise, so I figured we could easily take a week. I thought we'd spend a few days up at Yellowstone National Park, maybe catch a rodeo or go white water rafting."

"That sounds wonderful." Cassandra kissed him. "Are you all packed?"

"Mm-hm. I've been packed for two days. Good thing, too. I surely didn't have a chance to pack yesterday. How about you?"

"All I have to do is change."

"Me, too. Let's go."

Skip and Cassandra quietly slipped off to change out of their wedding clothes. Gently packing their fancy clothes in the rear of the trunk, Skip loaded Cassandra's suitcase on top of his. The newlyweds waved to everyone and left in Skip's car.

"Hey, Skip." Cassandra pulled a folded piece of printer paper from her pocket book and opened it. "I know it's out of the way, but could we make another stop first?"

Skip glanced over at her, then back at the road. "Sure. What's up?"

Cassandra sighed. "Well, yesterday, I got a letter from my uncle telling me that Sunset's been really sick, and she might not make it. Here, let me read it to you. 'Dear Cassie.' You know, Skip, I don't ever remember my uncle calling me Cassie."

"Really? Well, read me the letter."

"'Just thought I'd drop you a line and let you know that Sunset is terminally ill, and we don't expect her to live. I know how dearly you love that horse, her being your favorite, so I wanted to let you know so you can come see her before she passes away. Love, Uncle Woody.' Can we run down to my uncle's place? His ranch is about a half hour south of us."

"No problem." Skip made a u-turn. "How do I get there?"

"Go south on 487." Refolding the letter, Cassandra slipped it into her shirt pocket.

Skip followed the road beyond the city limits and turned right at a four-way stop.

Reaching into the back seat, Cassandra opened their ice chest and grabbed a canned soda. "You want one?"

"No, thanks. If I get thirsty, I'll have a sip of yours."

"All right. Oh, we need to turn here."

Skip completed a left-hand turn, drove past a no-trespassing sign and down a long winding driveway before finally reaching the house. Parking the car, he hastened around to open Cassandra's door. Cassandra grasped his hand and led the way to the front door, giving a hearty knock.

"Cassie, let me have a sip of your soda."

Cassandra handed him the can, and Skip took a swallow just as the door swung open. *Uncle Woody.*

Skip choked on the drink. Woody pounded him on the back, and Cassandra raised his arm above his head.

"You all right, son?"

Skip took a deep breath and nodded. But as his glance returned to Woody's face, his blue eyes widened in shock, and he slumped into a dead faint. Reacting quickly, Woody caught him.

"Cassandra, what in blazes is going on here?" The tall, handsome rancher lifted Skip into his strong arms. "Who is this boy?"

"Uncle Woody, this is my husband, Skip Shaughnessy."

Kicking the door shut, Cassandra followed her uncle into the house where he laid Skip on the sofa. Woody's wife, Mabel, a petite woman with graying, black hair, placed a cool compress on his forehead.

"Your husband?" said Mabel. "Did your mom finally approved of a boy, or did you elope?"

"She approved of him."

Woody embraced her. "Congratulations, darling. We're real happy for you. And we know if your mother approved of him, he's a champ. But what's wrong with him?"

"Nothing, Uncle Woody. I simply forgot to tell him that my dad has a twin brother."

"Cassandra, you are like our very own daughter. We love you dearly, and it broke our hearts when your mother no longer let you and Melanie come see us, but don't ever mention your father in this house again. I'm ashamed to be called his brother, let alone his twin. That man has dishonored the McKenzie name, and I want nothing to do with him."

"I'm sorry, Uncle Woody, but you have to explain it to Skip."

"Explain what to Skip?"

"That you are not my father, but his brother. Skip witnessed his father's murder and had to testify in court. The man he testified against was my father, and my dad threatened his life."

Mabel and Woody exchanged shocked looks.

"My father is in prison, but Skip doesn't know that he has a twin brother." Cassandra ran her fingers through his blond hair.

"Poor boy. No wonder he passed out," said Mabel.

Skip turned his head.

"He's stirring," whispered Mabel. "You'd better get out of sight, Woody."

Woody two-stepped out of the room.

Chapter 19

A Piece of Evidence

Bringing his hand to his head, Skip opened his eyes. "What happened? Cassandra?"

"Here I am, Angel." Cassandra caressed his cheek.

Skip removed the compress and sat up. Getting to his feet, he jammed trembling hands into his pockets and scanned the room for the assurance that he didn't really see what he thought he saw. Cassandra looped her arm through his, giving him a feeling of security.

"I'd like you to meet my Aunt Mabel."

"It's nice to meet you." Confident that he must have imagined it, Skip relaxed.

"Skip, there's something I forgot to tell you. My dad has a twin brother."

"A what?"

"A twin brother." Tightening her grip on his arm, Cassandra called out, "Uncle Woody."

Woody strolled out of the bedroom, and Skip jumped. Pulling away from Cassandra, he retreated.

"Relax, Skip. I don't bite." Woody approached him with long strides, extending his hand. "The name's John McKenzie, but I go by Woody. I'm Cassandra's Uncle."

Still in a state of shock, Skip only shook his hand to avoid appearing rude.

"Call me Uncle Woody."

Skip's eyes darted from Woody to Cassandra, but he didn't respond.

"So what brings you this way?" Woody asked Cassandra.

"You know why I'm here. I came to see Sunset."

"Sunset is terminally ill."

"I know. I wanted to see her before she died."

"Well, come on, then. She's resting in the barn."

Woody led the way outside, and Cassandra hurried after him, leaving Skip standing there. Skip didn't know if he should chase after her or wait for her to return. A moment later, she returned.

"Come on, Skip."

Grabbing his hand, she dragged him out the door and followed Woody to the barn. Cassandra escorted Skip into Sunset's stall.

The beautiful auburn horse, showing her age through streaks of gray, lay on her side, covered by a blanket.

"Oh, Sunset." Releasing Skip, Cassandra knelt beside the horse, gently stroking her long neck. Sunset nuzzled her.

"Hey, Cassandra, I think she remembers you," said Woody.

Rubbing the horse, Cassandra sighed. "She ought to remember me. Sunset was the only horse I ever rode. She was my favorite."

"She was? I didn't know that. How did you find out she was ill? Did Aunt Mabel write you?"

With raised eyebrows, Cassandra cocked her head. She looked at Skip and back at her uncle. "No, Uncle Woody." Pulling the letter from her shirt pocket, Cassandra handed it to him.

"What's this?" Woody opened it up and read it. "Cassandra, where did you get this?"

"It came in yesterday's mail."

"I did not write this. I didn't even know Sunset was your favorite. And I never call you 'Cassie.'"

Slowly rising, Cassandra stepped over to her uncle to see the note. Realizing the note was a ruse to draw them to Woody's ranch, and in light of the recent effort made to separate him and Cassandra, Skip now saw that note as a piece of evidence containing clues that could lead to the arrest of the men responsible for his kidnapping. That propelled him to Woody's side, and together they studied the note.

"There's no signature," said Skip. "The entire note has been typed, even your name."

"I'd like to know who sent this," exclaimed Woody.

Skip grasped the corner of the paper. "Well, whoever did it knows Sunset is ill. Sir, who knows the horse is ill?"

Raising an eyebrow, Woody looked at Skip. "Some of my ranch hands, but I guess they may have mentioned it to someone in town. I haven't any idea who knows."

"Whoever it is also knows that she's Cassandra's favorite."

"Hey, yeah," agreed Cassandra. "And it must be someone I know fairly well because they called me 'Cassie.'"

"Or else they think your uncle calls you 'Cassie.'"

"All right, you two detectives. Now, what was their reason?"

Skip and Cassandra looked at each other.

"Uncle Woody, that's a good question," said Cassandra.

A knock at the open barn door interrupted them. Everyone looked up from the note to a tall, muscular young man standing in the doorway with a pair of horse clipping shears in his hands.

"Mr. McKenzie, your wife said you were in the barn. I just stopped by to return your shears. Thanks for letting me borrow them."

"You're welcome, Doug." Woody took the shears from him.

Doug smiled at Cassandra. "Hey, what brings you here?"

"Sunset is going to die."

"That's too bad. I know how much you love her. Will you be staying for any length of time?"

"Well, we hadn't planned on it."

"We?"

Cassandra glowed. "This is my husband, Skip."

"You got married? Congratulations. I'm happy for you." Clasping Skip's hand firmly, Doug gave it a hearty shake. "Cassie is a wonderful girl."

Turning to Cassandra, Doug embraced her before heading toward the door.

"Well, I have to run. Mr. McKenzie, thanks again for the use of your shears." He waved. "Bye, Cassie. And good luck to both of you." With that, he disappeared out the barn door.

Skip looked at Cassandra. "Who is that?"

"Doug Benson. He's like my brother." Cassandra looked up at her uncle. "Uncle Woody, I didn't know that you and Doug were friends."

"Well ..." Pocketing the note and sliding his arms around Cassandra and Skip, Woody started walking back to the house. "I wouldn't exactly call us friends. I hardly know him. Occasionally, I run into him in the general store. He always asks about you, Cassandra."

"You hardly know him, yet you loaned him your shears?" asked Skip.

With a grin, Woody looked at him. "Yeah. He stopped by the other day and asked if he could borrow them to trim the forelock of his horses. He said they desperately needed a trim. Apparently, his brother, Dale, left his shears out in the rain, and they were rusted. Doug asked to borrow mine until he could replace his. Actually, I'm surprised he returned them so promptly."

Woody opened the front door and ushered Skip and Cassandra inside. "So, Cassandra, when did you get married?"

Cuddling up to Skip, Cassandra grinned. "This morning."

"This morning," said Mabel. "Shouldn't you kids be on your honeymoon?"

Cassandra gazed up at Skip. "We were headed to Yellowstone National Park for a few days. But I would enjoy it here just as much."

Looking around the large front room, Skip took note of everything. *Wow, this is a nice place.*

"Well, why don't you stay and visit for a few days," said Woody.

"We don't want to impose," said Cassandra.

Skip's eyes darted to Woody before he shifted his gaze. The man looked too much like Cassandra's dad for his peace of mind. So he appreciated her answer, because he *didn't* want to stay.

"Impose? You'd better impose. This whole place is going to belong to you kids, and you'd better know something about it."

"What are you talking about?" asked Cassandra. "What do you mean this whole place is going to belong to us?"

Skip raised an eyebrow at her question, but he looked the other way, feigning indifference to the discussion.

"Come now, Cassandra. You know that we never had any children of our own, so we think of you and Melanie like our daughters. This will all be yours one day. We've drawn up all the paperwork."

With a gasp, Cassandra clapped her hands together. "Ours?"

"You seem surprised. I wrote letters to you and Melanie and told you all about it," said Woody.

"You did? We never got them. Mom must have kept them from us."

Mabel rubbed her chin. "I'll bet we made the arrangements and wrote the letters after your dad went to trial. That's when your mother forbid us to see you."

"Well," said Woody. "I had this place assessed about four years ago. There are two houses on it, a couple of good-sized lakes, and a river that runs through it. Between the property and livestock, it's worth about three and a half million dollars."

Chapter 20

Looking at the Facts

Skip gasped. "Th-three and a half million dollars? Mr. McKenzie, who else knows this?"

"Just Mr. Osgood, the general store owner in town. You remember him, don't you, Cassandra?"

"Yes, very well. He's the nicest man."

"Sir, is it possible that he's told anyone else?"

Woody shook his head. "No. He's the only one in town I really talk to. And he never repeats anything. Good man, that Ben. He's a true friend. Every time I go into the store, he asks me if I've heard from the girls."

"Is anyone hungry?" asked Mabel.

"Not me. I'm full of cake. Aren't you, Skip?"

Skip shook his head. "No. I'm hungry."

"Smart boy," said Mabel. "And since the rest of us are eating, you may as well join us, Cassandra. You can't run all day on cake."

Cassandra sighed. "All right, Aunt Mabel."

"Good," said Woody. "While you two fix lunch, I want to talk to this boy alone for awhile. Come on, Skip. Let's take a walk."

Skip trailed Woody out the door. The man acted differently from Cassandra's father, but his remarkable resemblance caused Skip to maintain a healthy distance. Reaching the horse corral, Woody climbed onto the fence and sat down, so Skip did the same.

"Any boy that Anita lets near her daughter has got to be extra special," said Woody. "So tell me about yourself. What do you do for a living?"

"I'm a cop."

At that, Woody almost fell off the fence. "Does Anita know?"

"Yes, sir, she knows all about me." Skip surveyed the landscape while they talked.

"Skip, look at me," said Woody. "Look ... at ... me."

Skip's eyes met Woody's.

"I'm sorry for what happened to your dad. But I'm not Cassandra's father. That no good brother of mine is in prison, and I hope he rots there."

Skip started laughing.

"Well, don't you agree?" asked Woody.

"I couldn't agree more."

"I'm glad to finally see you smile. I was beginning to wonder about you."

Skip looked away. "I'm sorry. It's taken me a long time to get over the death of my father, and the sight of you was quite a shock."

"I'd imagine so."

"Dinner time," called Cassandra.

Skip and Woody hopped off the corral fence and started toward the house.

"You know how to ride a horse?" asked Woody.

"No, sir. Why do you ask?"

"You'd better learn if you hope to keep up with Cassandra."

Skip cringed at the thought. Images flashed through his mind of his nine-year-old classmate being bucked from a horse while on a fourth grade field trip to a farm. She broke her arm in two places. That could have happened to him. That should have happened to him. In line for a turn to ride, he allowed Ginny Beckman, who stood directly behind him, to go ahead of him. And she got thrown. None of the other children in line got their ride that day.

Trailing Woody into the house, Skip washed up before sitting down. Pondering everything that happened since the night of his abduction, he turned to Cassandra. "How long have you known Doug?"

"Oh, about ten years, I guess. My mom didn't approve of him. She always thought he was up to no good."

"Was he?"

"No. She thought that about every boy. Even you. Remember?"

Skip grinned. "All too well. Did you ever go riding with him?"

"Oh, yeah, all the time."

"So he knew that Sunset was your favorite horse."

"Of course. Skip, you don't honestly think that Doug is behind all this, do you?"

With a shrug, Skip emptied his glass of tea. "I don't know, Cassandra. I'm just looking at the facts. He called you 'Cassie,' like the writer of that note. And I firmly believe that the note is somehow tied in with everything else. Whoever wrote it knew you'd come here. Your uncle said that he hardly knew Doug when he asked to borrow the shears, so he was surprised that Doug returned them so promptly. Do you think it's coincidental that he happened to drop by while you were here?"

"It has to be. Skip, they caught the guys who abducted you."

"Yes, but they were all hired, and the guy who hired them was working with someone else. Whoever is responsible is well-acquainted with you."

"Maybe so, but it's not Doug," said Cassandra. "What's his motive?"

"Your inheritance."

"Don't be silly, Skip. Nobody knows about this inheritance except us and Mr. Osgood."

"That's right. Mr. Osgood, who runs the general store. And Mr. McKenzie, where did you see Doug?"

"Well, the general store, but ... Oh, no. Do you think he happened to overhear me telling Ben about our wills?"

"Unfortunately, I do."

"Well, I don't," said Cassandra. "Doug would never do such a thing, Skip. *Never.*"

"Do you know where he lives?" asked Skip.

Cassandra paused. "Yeah."

"Then let's run over and talk to him. See what he says."

"Well ..."

"Cassandra, I certainly hope you know me well enough to know that I would never railroad anyone."

"I know you wouldn't. We can go talk to him, if you'd like."

"If you're that certain that he's not involved, I'm inclined to follow your instincts, but I would feel better if I had a chance to talk to him."

"All right. We'll go to the Benson farm after dinner, but it's clear across town. I know a short cut if we go by horseback."

Skip winced, and fear gripped him.

Woody leaned over and whispered in his ear. "See what I mean?"

"See what you mean about what?" said Cassandra.

"Cassandra." Woody's voice was soft. "Has it not occurred to you that maybe this boy doesn't know how to ride a horse?"

"Oh, sure it has, so I asked his mother. She said that he's never been on a horse." Cassandra turned to Skip. "So I have a proposition for you."

Uh, oh. Skip wasn't sure he wanted to hear what she had to say.

"If you'll teach me how to drive the car, I'll teach you how to ride a horse."

I don't want to learn how to ride a horse. I'm afraid of falling. "L-l-lets just take the car."

"You're not willing to teach me how to drive?" Tears glistened in her eyes.

"Um ..." That did it. Now he made her cry. He didn't want to admit his reluctance to teach her to drive, but with her love for horses, she certainly wouldn't understand his fear, and she'd laugh at him. "Well, you don't have to shift a horse."

"Yeah, but you don't have to feed and water the car."

Skip swallowed hard. She had him cornered on both issues. And teaching her to drive a standard would be far easier than overcoming his fear and climbing onto a horse. But that's what he had to do.

Chapter 21

A Gathering of Evil Minds

Doug paced the floor of Kyle's apartment, not sure who to blame for this unfortunate turn of events. Kyle Carver and Rusty O'Sheif sat quietly at the small round dining room table.

"I hired you guys to ensure that Cassandra didn't get married. *To anyone.* What happened? She just introduced me to her husband."

"Have you ever gone rounds with that guy? He's a cop, and man can he fight," said Rusty.

"I don't care if he's a professional boxer. There were three of you."

"And the first time we grabbed him, it took all three of us to take him down."

"I don't believe it. He's not much bigger than my kid brother. And I've met Wayne. He's like a mountain."

"It's all blubber."

"Nevertheless, Rusty, you returned from Forest Valley and told me that you guys had dragged him a hundred miles from home, and although he'd escaped from you, he was still stranded, and there was no way he'd make it home in time for his wedding."

Rusty threw up his hands in frustration. "I'm sorry, Doug. We did our best. He must have caught a ride with someone. I don't know how else he got back in time."

Doug turned on Kyle. "You're awfully quiet."

"Just thinking. Rusty said Cassandra married a cop."

"So?"

"Dangerous line of work."

Jerking to a halt, Doug slid his hands in his pockets and grinned. "Yeah, it is. It would be a shame to see her widowed at such a young age. But she'd be available again. Wouldn't she?"

Doug glanced at his watch. "Whoa, is it late. I got to get back to the farm and get that money to the bank before it closes."

"What money?" asked Kyle.

Doug laughed. "The hundred grand I scammed off that dingbat who thinks I'm her friend. She cleaned out her savings account and gave it to me yesterday morning to invest for her."

Kyle's eyes widened, and Rusty's mouth dropped open.

"A hundred grand?" gasped Rusty.

"I'm investing it, all right. And I'm not sharing," said Doug. "We've worked hard on our little business venture, and we're splitting that three ways, but this money is mine. I've stashed it in the library because Dale can't go in there. That way, he won't stumble upon it by accident."

"When are we getting out of here, Doug?" asked Rusty. "Things are getting hot."

"We'll wrap things up by the weekend and be out of here next week."

"You leaving Cassandra then?" asked Kyle.

"Not if I can help it. I'm gonna think of a way to get rid of her husband."

"Good luck with that," said Rusty.

"What about your kid brother?"

"He'll be on his own." Snatching up his cowboy hat, Doug headed for the door. "Be at my place first thing in the morning. I'll send Dale on an errand to get rid of him. Then we'll empty the basement of that stolen merchandise. I know where we can go to sell it, and it'll bring us top dollar. It'll give us loads of spending cash for our trip to Australia."

Chapter 22

A Ride on Cupcake

Skip started to clear his plate, but Mabel stopped him. "I'll do that. You kids run along."

Woody walked them to the door. "Hold on, Cassandra. Before you go, we have to know if you're staying."

Cassandra looped her arm through Skip's and snuggled up to him. "I'd like to. Skip?"

Skip glanced from Mabel to Woody. "Well, I ..."

Bursting into laughter, Woody pulled him off to the side and lowered his voice. "Skip, we have the nicest little guest cabin around back. You and Cassandra would have it all to yourselves."

"Thank you, sir. Then, we'll stay."

"Great." Woody looked pleased. "Now, why don't you change before you go. You don't want to wear those good clothes over to the Bensons' farm, especially if you're going by horseback."

Skip slid his hands into his pockets. "Oh. All I have is dress slacks."

"You don't have any blue jeans?"

"No, sir."

"Cassandra, is he joking?"

"Afraid not, Uncle Woody. Skip doesn't like the feel of denim."

"Hm." Woody looked at Skip. "You'd better learn to like the feel of them if you're going to spend much time out here. Come with me. I have a brand new pair of bib overalls that Mabel bought me, and they don't fit me. They ought to fit you fine. You can have them."

Skip followed Woody back to the bedroom. Woody pulled out the overalls and thrust them into his hands. The denim felt stiff and abrasive.

"What's the matter?"

"They're rough."

Woody laughed. "Of course, they're rough. They're made to be rough. You sound like you're always around girls. Girls like softness. Now, put them on, and don't be a sissy."

"I'm not a sissy," Skip yelled as Woody strolled out and shut the door.

Skip stripped off his good trousers and slipped into the overalls, tucking in his collared shirt and snapping the straps. "Oo, I like these pockets." He slid his hands into the big roomy pockets and hurried out the front door. Cassandra and Woody stood by the car, waiting for him.

"Mabel will have the cabin ready for you when you get back. By the way, Cassandra, are you going by horseback?"

Skip cringed at the thought.

"Yes, Uncle Woody, if it's all right with you."

"Sure is. Let me saddle you up two horses."

"Wait. C-c-can't I ride with Cassandra?"

"Skip," said Cassandra. "Don't be silly."

"That might be a little hard on the horse to carry two adults," said Woody. He motioned for Skip to join him. "Come help me saddle them."

Woody headed into the corral and rounded up two horses. Skip followed him, and Cassandra climbed onto the fence to wait.

Leading the horses over to Skip, Woody smiled at him. "Skip, this is Lightning." Woody patted the black and white horse. "She's a runner. Believe me, she lives up to her name. We'll give her to Cassandra."

Skip looked at the other horse. Her coat was silky brown.

"This is Cupcake." Woody stroked her. "She's very gentle. You'll like her."

"Sh-she doesn't buck?"

"No. She moves gracefully and slowly. She's perfect for your very first time on a horse."

Skip reached out and petted the horse.

Walking alongside Skip, Woody slowly led the horses toward the barn to saddle them. Cassandra hopped off the fence and started to follow them. "Cassandra, you wait there. Skip and I will saddle Lightning and bring her out to you."

"Oo, thank you." Cassandra climbed back onto the corral fence.

Woody escorted Skip into the barn and led the horses over to the shelf that held the saddles. Hoisting a saddle onto Cupcake, Woody securely fastened it in place.

"Now, Lightning will want to run. And Cassandra will want to race. But Cupcake won't take off with you on her back, and she won't buck you off. She's a good horse. You want to give her a try?"

Skip knew that the best way to overcome a fear was to face it, but he glanced around the barn, not sure he was ready to face this fear. While he thought about it, Woody saddled Lightning for Cassandra.

Skip felt no pressure from Woody. He liked that. But he had to decide, and right now he could use a little guidance in making this decision. He drew in a deep breath and looked over at the open barn door. Cassandra was waiting on him. Plus, he had to go see Doug Benson.

With Lightning saddled, Woody looked at him. "Skip, would you like me to drive you over there in the car? Cassandra can still take Lightning and meet us there."

Skip paused. "Um ... w-w-well ..."

"Why don't you climb on and get the feel. Then you can decide."

Woody instructed him on how to properly mount the horse. Once Skip was in the saddle, Woody led Cupcake around the barn.

Skip relaxed. This wasn't hard at all. What was he afraid of?

"You think you'll be all right?"

"Yes, sir. Thanks for understanding. I don't think Cassandra would have."

"No," said Woody. "That's why I had her wait at the corral."

Standing beside Cupcake, Woody gave Skip some basic instructions on how to guide the horse, get her moving, and gently stop her. "Now, if she's in the mood, she will run, but not unless you tell her to."

Stepping into the stirrup, Woody swung himself onto Lightning's back. "Let's go out to Cassandra. She's probably wondering what's taking us so long."

Sitting on Cupcake, Skip followed Woody out the door and over to Cassandra. Woody swung himself down and handed Cassandra the reigns.

"Thanks, Uncle Woody." Cassandra climbed into the saddle. "Why don't you come with us?"

"I'd like to, honey, but I have things to take care of here."

Cassandra released a sigh of disappointment. "I understand."

"Now, Cassandra, Skip may be a fast learner, but please remember that he's an inexperienced rider. This is his very first time on a horse, so absolutely no racing. You allow him to go at a pace he's comfortable with. I don't want him to fall and get hurt."

Skip found the clip-clop of the horses hooves somewhat melodious, so he couldn't help but relax. But while Cupcake seemed content to walk, Lightning was starting to get antsy, so Cassandra allowed her to trot.

"Hey, Skip, I'll race you to that tree over there." Letting Lightning canter, Cassandra rode on ahead.

That tree over there? Which one? There were lots of trees.

When Cassandra disappeared from view, Skip slowed Cupcake to a stop, fighting the sudden panic that surfaced within him. He glanced around, looking for Cassandra.

"Cassandra, don't do this to me." He spoke softly, more to himself than to her. Looking around again, he realized he had no idea which direction they'd come from and which direction to go. They weren't following a trail or a pathway. They were cutting across a field with rocks and trees everywhere.

Skip patted the horse. "Cupcake, I'm lost and have no idea which way she went. Do you know?"

With a whinny, the horse nodded.

"Good girl. Just follow her." Skip nudged Cupcake forward. Feeling comfortable with her steady gait, he felt ready to handle a trot, so he urged her to go a little faster. *Lord, did I just ask directions from a horse?*

"*Boo.*" Cassandra rode up behind him.

Skip jumped and almost fell off Cupcake. "That wasn't nice, Cassandra." Struggling to regain his balance, he once more slowed her to a walk.

Cassandra giggled at him. "I'm sorry. I shouldn't have done that. I didn't realize it would startle you. Now Doug lives just over that hill. I'll race you." Cassandra snapped the reins and off she flew. *"I won."*

Skip's horse plodded toward her. "Congratulations."

"Aw, Skip, that race was no fun. You didn't even try to win,"

"What can I say? Cupcake didn't feel like racing."

"Hey, what's going on over here?" called another rider. Doug Benson rode up to them on a beautiful black stallion. "Howdy, Cassie. What brings you guys out here?"

"I'm teaching Skip to ride a horse."

"Way out here?"

"Sure, and we thought we'd stop by to say 'hi' if that's all right."

"Absolutely. I was on my to the bank, but I can go tomorrow."

Skip grinned. Cassandra opened the door for him to casually question Doug.

Joining Cassandra, Doug's horse trotted alongside hers. Doug ignored Skip as if he weren't there.

"Let's put the horses in the barn, and we'll go into the house for a cold drink."

"Thanks, Doug, we'd love to," said Cassandra.

Breaking their horses into a gallop, Doug and Cassandra raced off, leaving Skip on his own. Cupcake followed them at a leisurely pace, and Skip felt no need to hurry, so he let her walk. They'd eventually get there.

A Way to Escape

As they crested the top of the hill, Skip saw the farmhouse down in the valley and the barn on the other side of it. Cassandra and Doug had dismounted their horses and were walking together.

Feeling forgotten and abandoned by his young bride on the very day they were starting their lives together, Skip was beginning to think that he should have let her go. But he loved her, and at the time, he thought she loved him.

She loves Doug Benson. She only married me because her mom didn't approve of Doug.

Caught in a Lie

"That was fun," said Cassandra, strolling alongside Doug to the barn. "I haven't had a chance to ride like that in years, and I'm already starting to feel it. Boy, am I going to be sore tomorrow."

"Shall we settle the horses in the barn and go into the house for a cold drink?"

"We will, when Skip gets here. This is his very first time on a horse, so he's not comfortable going fast, yet. But before long, he'll start picking up speed."

Seeing Skip and Cupcake traipsing toward them, Cassandra grinned and waved. "Come on, Skip, we're waiting for you."

As Skip approached them, Cassandra left Doug and ran to greet him. "Sorry for galloping off, but Lightning was itching to run, and I was itching to race, so I took advantage of the opportunity Doug gave me to have a riding companion." Reaching up, she clasped his hand. "I hope you didn't mind. I look forward to the day that you're my riding companion."

With a smile, Skip climbed off the horse. His legs ached from that long ride. Pulling Cassandra into his arms, he whispered in her ear. "Is that all it was?"

With a smile, Cassandra kissed him. "That's all. Now let's put the horses in the barn and go get a drink."

Leading their horses toward the barn, they joined Doug and followed him through the huge double doors.

"Hey, Cassandra."

Cassandra looked up at the hayloft. "Hi, Dale. Boy, have you grown. This is my husband, Skip. Skip, this is Dale, Doug's younger brother."

Dale grabbed a rope and swung down like Tarzan. "Pleased to meet you." He extended his hand.

Grasping his hand, Skip studied him. He was a couple of years younger than Cassandra, tall and lanky, but he guessed Doug to be in his early twenties, built more like a football player.

"Come over to the house," said Dale, heading out the barn door.

Skip grasped Cassandra's hand, observing their surroundings as they followed Dale. He noticed a pair of horse clipping shears hanging neatly on the wall near several other tools. They obviously weren't new, but neither were they rusted.

Doug trailed them into the house. "Make yourselves comfortable. I'll be right back with our drinks." Seizing his brother by the shirt, he dragged Dale into the kitchen and closed the door.

A minute later, Dale re-entered the living room, slightly peaked. Doug followed him through the door with four full glasses of lemonade on a carrying tray.

"Come and get it." He set the tray on the coffee table.

Dale handed him a glass. "Here, Skip."

"Thanks, Dale." Skip graciously accepted it, wondering how he could dump it out without anyone noticing.

Dale put his finger to his lips and motioned for Skip to follow him. While Doug and Cassandra were chatting, the boys slipped into the kitchen and emptied their glasses into the sink.

"Don't you like lemonade, either?" asked Skip.

"No, I can't stand it, but my brother is so stubborn that I can't get it through to him. He thinks everybody ought to like it." Dale opened the refrigerator door and snatched out a cream soda. "What would you like? We're stocked on soda."

"You got Root Beer?"

"You'd better believe it." Snatching out a canned Root Beer, Dale tossed it to Skip.

Skip caught the can and popped the top open.

It thrilled Cassandra to be able to catch up with the Benson brothers because she hadn't seen them in years. They were so much a part of her childhood that she thought of them as her brothers.

Doug grasped her hand. "Cassie, come with me. I have something special to show you." He hustled her outside.

"Something special?" Excitement swelled up within her.

Holding her hand, Doug led her back into the barn. "Remember all the fun we had riding together?"

"Oh, yeah. It's part of my childhood I will always cherish. You and Dale are just like my brothers."

"Well, I like you a lot. You're more to me than a sister."

"I am?"

"Mm-hm." Reaching up, Doug lifted his shiny leather saddle off a high shelf and set it on a table for Cassandra to see. Gold trim circled the saddle while shimmering gold lettering spelled Cassandra's name on one side and his name on the other.

"Oh, Doug, it's beautiful, but why did you put my name on it?"

"Cassie, you've always been my girl. Why did you marry ..." Doug cleared his throat before nodding toward the house. "... him?"

Cassandra's smile quickly faded. "You sound jealous."

Doug shrugged. "I guess, I am. I love you, Cassandra. I've always loved you. And I thought you loved me." Doug stepped closer to her, and Cassandra slowly backed away.

"I'm so sorry, Doug. I didn't know you felt that way about me. I never intended to mislead you."

"It's all right." Glancing around nonchalantly, Doug slid his hands in his pockets and stepped closer to her.

Taking another step backward, Cassandra grinned nervously and wrung her hands. "I wonder what Skip's doing." She tried to hide the tremor in her voice. "Let's go see."

Cassandra started toward the door, but Doug grabbed her arm. "Wait. I know you're married and that you're a girl of good character and virtue, so I want you to make me a promise."

"Boy, it's quiet in the other room," said Skip. Setting his can on the counter, he hurried into the living room. "Where did they go?"

Dale shrugged. "I don't know. Doug told me to keep you busy so he could talk to Cassandra in private, but he didn't say anything about them leaving the room. Maybe they stepped outside."

"Cassandra," Skip hollered up the stairs. No answer. "Hm, let's go see if they went outside." Skip hustled out the front door, hurriedly looking around. "Cassandra!"

Hearing Skip call her, Cassandra turned to answer him, but Doug squeezed her arm. "Shh, Cassie, don't panic. Just make me a simple promise."

"What kind of promise?"

"Well, if for some reason things don't work out between you and Skip, or if something should happen to him, I want you to promise that you'll come here, and I'll take care of you."

"Doug," gasped Cassandra.

"Please, promise me, because no one has a guarantee for tomorrow. And since Skip is a cop, he ..."

"How did you know that?"

"Uh, how did I know what?"

"That Skip is a police officer."

Doug loosened his grip on Cassandra's arm. "You told me."

"No, I didn't. So how did you know? Are you in some way responsible for hampering our wedding plans?"

"Don't be ridiculous."

"Well, are you?" demanded Cassandra.

"Cassandra!" Skip's voice grew louder, and she knew that he was headed toward the barn.

"Look, Cassie, I truly love you and would never do anything to hurt you. But sometimes things happen, and I want to make sure you're taken care of. So promise me that if anything happens to Skip, you'll come back here and marry me. I love you more than you'll ever know."

"I can't make that kind of promise."

"Why not?"

"Because I'm not in love with you."

Doug squeezed her arm again.

"Ow! Doug, you're hurting me." Cassandra struggled to break free.

"Promise me, and I'll let you go." His iron grip tightened even more.

"Doug Benson, you let me go this minute, or so help me, you'll regret it." Cassandra kicked him in the shin and slammed her fist on his forearm, but Doug's grip was too strong to break. "Skip!"

Racing into the barn, Skip slugged Doug in the jaw, forcing him to release Cassandra. "I'm tired of playing your game, Benson. Don't touch my wife!"

Cassandra scrambled behind Skip for protection. Dale joined her.

Doug rubbed his jaw. "Yeah, I guess I was a little out of line." He extended his hand in a friendly gesture. "Truce?"

Skip paused.

Despite what Doug had just done to her, Cassandra still hoped that he and Skip could be friends, so she smiled when they shook hands. But she cringed when Doug torpedoed his left fist at Skip's head.

Leaping to the left, Skip promptly raised Doug's right arm, deflecting the blow, and turned his clasped hand, positioning his on top. Cocking it upward, he forced Doug's wrist into a joint lock, bending his fingers back and raising him up on his toes.

"Ah! Stop! That hurts."

Skip released Doug and reached for Cassandra's hand. "Are you all right?" Holding hands, they left the barn.

"Skip, look out!" cried Dale.

Doug tackled Skip and slugged him. Cassandra screamed. On the ground, Skip drove his elbow into

Doug's mid section, rolling out from under him, but Doug wasn't about to let him go. He dived on Skip, attempting to pin him down. Arching his back and rolling, Skip bucked him off, clocking him in the eye with his fist and rolling on top of him.

Dale jerked Cassandra away from the fistfight.

"Stop it!" Cassandra watched Doug and Skip rolling on the ground slugging it out.

Dale, on the other hand, was jumping up and down, swinging his arms like he were involved in the brawl. "Give him a right!" He swung his right arm. "And a left!" He swung his left arm. "Knock his block off!" He swung his right arm again. "Pound him good!" He brought both fists down like he was pounding someone over the head.

"Dale, what are you saying? Leave him alone, Doug!"

Doug scrambled onto Skip, attempting to pin him to the ground. Leaping onto Doug's back, Cassandra grasped the back of his shirt.

"Cassandra, no!" Dale yanked her off his brother and pulled her away from them. Skip lost his glasses as they rumbled, so Dale snatched them up and hastily retreated. "Here, Cassandra. I don't think they're damaged."

Cassandra snatched them away from him. "Fine friend you are. Why don't you do something?"

"I am. I'm cheering. But don't worry, if Skip kills him, we'll both testify it was self defense."

Chapter 24

A Hint of Animosity

Leaping to his feet, Skip decided to bring this fight to a quick end. Deflecting Doug's right punch with the back of his right hand, Skip grabbed his wrist and smashed his elbow with his left hand.

"Ah!"

Doug felt that. Seizing his wrist with both hands, Skip jerked him forward, grabbed the back of his shoulder and pulled him down while raising his right arm. Skip bent his arm and shoved him face down on the ground, holding him securely in a hammerlock.

Doug groaned. "Okay, I give up. You win. Now get off me before you break my arm."

"Dale, bring me some rope."

"No." Doug struggled to escape Skip's grasp. "Don't tie me up. *No.*"

Taking the rope from Dale, Skip securely bound Doug's hands behind his back.

"Dale, stop him."

Dale dropped on his knees beside his brother. "Why should I? After they leave, I know you'll pound me."

"You mean, you were rooting for Skip to win that fight? Dale, when I get loose, you've had it."

"Uh, oh." Dale rose to his feet and backed away. "Can I go with you guys? I don't want to be around when he gets loose."

"He's not getting loose, but you can come with us." Skip searched Doug, removing a small spiral notebook from his hip pocket.

"Hey, that's private."

Skip opened it and grinned. "I can see that." Folding the notebook, he slipped it into his bib pocket and stood. "Come on, Cassandra. We have what we came for."

While Dale and Cassandra mounted their horses, Skip brushed off his overalls. Sore and stiff from his first horseback ride, he climbed back into the saddle and grimaced at the discomfort.

"If you leave with them, you're dead meat, Dale."

"You'll be safe with us, Dale," said Skip. They waved at Doug as they rode off.

"I'll get you for this, Dale. Mark my words."

Dale glanced back at his brother, but kept going.

Leaving Doug tied up like he did, Skip wondered if he should try to pick up his return pace just a little. He and Cupcake were meandering home as slowly as they plodded out there. Riding in the middle, Skip glanced from Dale to Cassandra. They seemed perfectly content to slow their pace for him.

Skip looked at Dale. "Thanks for pulling Cassandra out of danger and rescuing my glasses. Do you mind if I ask how old you are?"

"Sixteen."

"Where are your parents?" asked Skip.

"They died a couple years ago, so it's just me and Doug."

"You two run the farm by yourselves?"

"Hm-hm."

"Have you ever considered what you would do if anything happened to your brother?"

Dale shook his head. "I guess I'd have to quit school and work the farm full time. I'm trying to figure out what I'm going to do now. Doug's got a vicious temper and I'm afraid to go home. But I have to. I don't have any place else to go and somebody's got to untie him."

"Don't worry about Doug. I'm taking the sheriff back out there with me, and we'll take care of him. I'm concerned about you."

Dale shrugged. "I'll be all right. Doug will get over his anger eventually."

"That's not what I meant," said Skip. "Dale, you need to know, so I might as well tell you now. Your brother has done some illegal things and will likely go to prison."

"Why does that not surprise me? But how do you know that?"

"It's a long story. I'll tell you about it later. I guess I should see if I can get Cupcake to pick up her pace. Doug is tied up back there."

"Don't hurry to rescue him on my account," said Cassandra. "As far as I'm concerned, you can take the sheriff out there after we've eaten supper."

Skip looked at her. "Oo, do I detect a hint of animosity in your tone?"

"No, you detect *a lot* of animosity in my tone."

As they plodded toward the house, Woody hurried to meet them. "Skip, are you all right?" With one hand on his arm and the other on his back, Woody helped him climb down off the horse while Dale and Cassandra dismounted. "You landed in a fistfight with Doug, didn't you? I never should have let you kids go out there alone. I've heard that Doug will start a fight over almost anything. I just didn't know how true it was."

"Mr. McKenzie, I'm going to shower and clean up. Then I need to go into town to see the sheriff, if you'll tell me how to get there."

"No problem. Just go around back. Mabel has the cabin all cleaned up for you kids. It has a shower in it. I hauled your suitcases into it already."

"How did you get to them? They were locked in the trunk of the car."

With a grin, Woody held up Skip's keys. "Found them in your pants pocket."

"Oh, thanks. I didn't even miss them."

Taking his keys, Skip hustled to the cabin around back and hurried to shower and change. When he finished, he dressed neatly in khaki trousers and a short-sleeve plaid shirt. After combing his hair and cleaning his glasses, he returned to the house and quietly entered.

Woody jumped to his feet. "Skip, you ready to go into town?"

"Yes, sir. How do I get there?"

"I want to go," said Cassandra.

"I'd rather you didn't. I don't want you to see us arrest your old friend."

"I won't be any trouble. I've just got to go."

"Me, too!" said Dale.

Skip sighed. "All right."

"I'm taking you this time," said Woody. "Mabel, we're going into town."

"Would you stop by the general store and pick me up some flour?"

"Sure, dear." Woody swung open the front door. "Oh, and Dale's eating supper with us tonight."

Dale and Cassandra dashed past Woody and raced out to the car, but Woody stopped Skip at the door.

"Skip, call me Woody. Understand?"

"Yes, sir."

"You don't mind if I call you 'son,' do you?"

"No, sir, I like it."

"Good. I've always wanted a boy, and it'll be easy to think of you as my own. Let's go, son."

Leading the way out the door, Skip slid behind the wheel, and Woody slid in beside him. Then they took off for town. Their first stop was the general store to pick up the flour. While Woody paid for the flour, Skip looked around the store.

"Woody, if you stood there at the counter talking to Mr. Osgood, Doug could have been lingering in here almost anywhere, and you would not have known that someone was listening to everything you said."

Woody glanced around the store. "You're right."

"Woody, who is this boy? Some sort of detective?"

"No. This is Cassandra's husband. Come on, Skip. We need to get over to see the sheriff before he goes home for the day. Talk to you later, Ben."

Skip and Woody hurried back to the car and drove to the sheriff's office. Within ninety minutes of the time he'd left the Benson farm, Skip returned with the graying sheriff. Doug was nowhere around. Parking the vehicles, everyone piled out.

Sheriff Kasey Robins spoke softly to Woody, Dale, and Cassandra. "Okay, you three wait by the vehicles. Dale, I want you to call out loudly to Doug."

"I'm home, Doug," called Dale. "Where are you?"

"Well, it's about time, you little traitor. Now, come untie me."

His voice came from the house. With their guns ready, Skip and the sheriff slowly approached the house.

Chapter 25

Making Decisions

Skip crept around to the back of the house, ducking under windows while Sheriff Robins covered the front.

"Hey, Dale, get in here, and untie me."

In position, Skip waited for the sheriff's signal. At the sound of a loud whistle, he burst through the back door, meeting the other officer in the living room as they converged on Doug simultaneously, two guns pointed at him.

"Don't move, Benson," ordered Sheriff Robins.

Seeing Doug still bound by the rope, Skip started laughing and re-holstered his gun.

"You've got a lot of nerve bringing the sheriff here after doing this to me. Sheriff, I want him arrested for trespassing, assault and battery, and kidnapping my brother."

"You do, huh? Well, save your complaints. You can tell them to the judge. Now, let's go."

Grasping Doug's arms, Skip and the sheriff led him out to the patrol car.

"Aren't you going to untie me?"

"No. It's either that or handcuffs. And I believe that Officer Shaughnessy did a first rate job of tying you up."

As they approached the sheriff's car, Doug looked at Cassandra. "How could you do this to me?" he said, scooting into the back seat of the cruiser.

"Doug, I love you. I've loved you for years. You're like my big brother. How could you hurt me like you did? How could you be responsible for the threats and kidnapping and attempted murder of my fiance?"

Pursing his lips, Doug looked away.

"Thank you, Skip." Sheriff Robins shook his hand. "If ever I can do anything for you, give me a call. It's been a pleasure working with an officer of the Forest Valley Police Department."

"Thank you, sir." With an impish grin, Skip winked at Doug and waved at him as the police car drove away.

Woody slid his arm around Dale. "Well, son, what are we going to do with you and the farm?"

"I guess I'll have to quit school. Somebody has to take care of the animals."

"That's true, but this is too big a job for a 16-year-old. And *you* need your education. Why don't we put the farm up for sale, and you can come live with us."

"Do you mean it?"

"You bet I do. I can't get over how the Lord works. Just yesterday, Mabel and I were on our knees praying that God would send us some children. Mabel wants a daughter, and I want a son, and here God's given me two." He slid his arms around Dale and Skip.

"Oh, Uncle Woody, don't be silly. We're not children," said Cassandra.

"Cassandra, how old are you?"

"Eighteen."

"Okay, and Dale is sixteen. And Skip is only nineteen. He won't turn twenty until next week."

"How'd you know that?" asked Skip.

Woody blushed. "You also left your wallet in your pants pocket."

"Oops."

"Mabel and I are nearing fifty, and you're all kids to us. Now, Cassandra, I know that your mother loves you very much, but you don't have a dad at home. And neither one of these boys even has a dad any more, so you are all hereby declared my children. What do you say?"

"I'm hungry, Dad," said Dale.

"Dale, have all the animals been taken care of for today?" asked Woody.

"Yes, sir."

"Good. Go throw together a bag with some clothes and personal hygiene items. Then we'll go home and eat."

Dale spun around and dashed off.

Woody turned to Skip. "As for you, young man. Tomorrow, get yourself some jeans."

Skip grimaced. "I don't like them. They're rough."

"Don't buy the rough ones. Buy soft denim. You'll like the feel of them. Then leave them at our place when you leave. That way, when you come to visit, you'll always have appropriate clothes. But buy yourself some jeans."

"Yes, sir."

Sitting at the table gazing at Skip, Cassandra rubbed his back. He could hardly keep his eyes open at the dinner table.

Skip stifled a yawn. "I'm sorry. I didn't get any sleep last night, and it's catching up with me."

"Come on, Angel." Cassandra stood, grasped his arm, and helped him to his feet. "Let's get you to bed. Aunt Mabel, I'll be back to help with dishes."

"You'll do nothing of the kind. Dale can help me. This is your wedding night. Spend it with your husband."

"Thanks, Aunt Mabel. Good night, everyone. See y'all in the morning."

Skip yawned. Removing his glasses, he rubbed his eyes. Cassandra slid her arm around him and escorted him out the back door and up the walkway into the small cabin.

Skip dropped onto the bed, unbuttoning his shirt and sliding it off. "I'm so tired, and boy am I sore. That guy hit hard." He collapsed onto the bed on his stomach.

Skip's steady breathing indicated he was out. After removing his shoes and covering him with a blanket, Cassandra crawled in beside him. She breathed a contented sigh as she caressed his silky blond hair and slid her hand underneath his tee shirt to rub his smooth back. She finally had the freedom to stay with him as long as she wanted – to touch him as much as she wanted, anywhere she wanted.

Pacing the floor with the telephone to his ear, Rusty listened to the continuous ringing. He'd been trying to reach Doug for over an hour. He finally disconnected the call and dialed Kyle's number. "Have you talked to Doug this evening?"

"No. I've been busy booking our flights to Australia."

"Well, I've been trying to reach him for almost ninety minutes. His phone just rings. He's not answering. His kid brother isn't answering. Something's wrong."

"They're probably at the movies. If I were you, I'd start packing. Tomorrow morning, we're helping Doug take care of the rest of our merchandise. Then we're out of here."

Chapter 26

In Need of Security

Streaming through the window, the sunlight roused Skip from a sound sleep. Bruised and sore, he slapped his hand over his eyes and slowly sat up on the bed.

He tossed the blanket aside and felt around for his dark glasses, finally locating them on the nightstand beside the bed.

With some relief from the bright sun, he pulled on his shoes and a fresh shirt. Then he ran a wet comb through his hair before leaving the cabin. Skip squinted while shielding his eyes with his left hand. He followed the walkway that led from the cabin to the house and knocked on the back door.

Aunt Mabel swung open the door. "Skip, you don't have to knock. Just walk in. You belong here. You hungry?" Aunt Mabel escorted him into the dining room, talking as they walked. "Sit down and I'll bring you some lunch."

"Lunch?" Skip glanced at his watch. It was almost eleven o'clock. "W-where is everybody?"

"Woody is out in the north forty, tending the cattle. Dale and Cassandra took off early this morning for the farm. Until we sell it, somebody will have to go out there every morning to feed the animals, milk the cows, and do the chores."

"Boy, I hadn't thought about that." Skip slid onto a hardback dining room chair.

Mabel laughed as she prepared his lunch. "That's cause you're a city kid."

"But to unload that responsibility on a sixteen-year-old ..." Skip's mind flew back to the death of his dad. He was only sixteen when he assumed the role of provider for his family and father figure to his little sisters.

"We'll make sure he has help, especially come fall, when he's back in school. Don't worry about Dale. He's used to hard work. I'm just sorry that he had to see his brother get arrested. There's been a rash of thefts around town and the sheriff suspected Doug. He just didn't have any proof."

"What kind of thefts?"

"Mostly electronics."

"Why didn't the sheriff obtain a search warrant for his property?"

Mabel set Skip's plate in front of him and sat down beside him. "He did, but they didn't find anything.

Sheriff Robins was convinced that Doug was the culprit, so he's grateful for your assistance in getting him off the street, even if his arrest was for a different reason. He stopped by last night to thank you, but you were already asleep."

"What time did Dale and Cassandra leave?"

"About seven. They wanted to wake you, but I wouldn't let them. Tomorrow, you're on your own."

Skip and Aunt Mabel chatted while he ate his lunch. Shoveling in the last bite, Skip pushed himself away from the table and deposited his plate in the sink.

"That was delicious, Aunt Mabel. Thank you. May I use the telephone to call home? I want to give my mom a number to reach me in case of an emergency."

"You go ahead, sweetheart."

Skip scooped up the receiver and punched in his home phone number.

"Skip, don't tell me that you're homesick all ready? You only left yesterday," teased his mother.

"Not hardly. But I wanted to leave you with a phone number where you can reach me in case of an emergency."

"An emergency, huh?"

"Yeah. What's the matter? Is something wrong?"

Erin sighed. "Yes, but I would hardly consider it an emergency."

"What is it?"

"It's Stephanie. Ever since you and Cassandra left yesterday, she's done nothing but cry. She won't eat. She won't talk. She won't play."

"That's not like Stephanie," said Skip. "This sounds serious. Go pack her a suitcase, and I'll be home in an hour to get her."

"Oh, Skip, you and Cassandra are on your honeymoon. You've only been married for twenty four hours."

"Don't worry about us. We're visiting Cassandra's aunt and uncle at their ranch. They'd enjoy having Stephanie, and Cassandra and I will have plenty of time together."

"All right, honey, if you're sure."

"I am, Mom. And don't tell her I'm coming. See you soon." Skip hung up the telephone and smiled at Mabel.

"How old is Stephanie?"

"She's almost ten."

"I'll have a room ready for her when you get back."

"Thanks, Aunt Mabel." He kissed her on the cheek and headed out the door to the car.

Uncertain when Dale and Cassandra would return, Skip didn't wait. With his window down, he enjoyed the warm breeze on the drive home. Within an hour, he entered the house.

"Mom?" He peeked into each room. Boy, was the house quiet. Where was everybody? Skip started up the stairs.

Erin emerged from Stephanie's bedroom with a suitcase in her hand. She met him halfway down the steps and handed it to him.

Skip grasped the suitcase handle. "Where are the girls?

"Cassandra's sister took the younger three to the park, but Stephanie's down in the basement."

"In the basement? Doing what?"

"Go see."

Skip jogged to the car and tossed Stephanie's small suitcase into the trunk. Trotting back into the house, he passed through the kitchen to the closed basement door. He quietly turned the knob and pulled open the door. There sat Stephanie, halfway down the steps, staring into space. Skip softly descended the steps and sat beside his younger sister. When Stephanie didn't look at him, he slid his arm around her shoulders and hugged her.

"Hey, talk to me."

"Skip?" Stephanie turned and her mouth fell open. "Oh, Skip!"

Flinging her arms around his neck, Stephanie buried her face in his shirt and burst into tears. Skip embraced her for several minutes, letting her cry.

"Come on, Stephanie. Let's go for a ride." Grasping her hand, he guided her back up the stairs and closed the basement door. "Bye, Mom." He kissed Erin on the cheek. "We're leaving."

Erin embraced her daughter. "Be good for your brother, Stephanie."

Stephanie nodded. She followed Skip outside. He opened the door for her, and she climbed into the front passenger seat. Skip slid behind the wheel and cranked the engine. They were halfway back to the ranch when Stephanie finally broke the silence.

"Mom called you and told you to come get me. Didn't she?"

"Nope, it was my idea. She did tell me that you've been rather moody lately. Do you want to tell me about it?"

"I don't see what good it will do. You're going away, just like Daddy did."

Skip raised an eyebrow. "Is that why you've been so upset? You think I'm gonna die?"

"No, Skip. Dad went to Heaven to live with Jesus, and now that you're married, you're going to move away to live with Cassandra. And you're all the daddy I have. I don't want you to go away!" Stephanie burst into fresh tears.

Chapter 27

Strange Happenings

Skip squeezed her hand. "Stephanie, what makes you think I'm moving away?"

"The Bible says that a man is to leave his father and mother and cleave unto his wife."

"That's true, but the Bible also tells me to take care of my widowed mother."

"So you're not leaving?"

"Not for awhile."

Stephanie smiled, but her smile faded. "H-h-how long awhile?"

Skip patted her hand. "Now, that I can't answer, but don't you worry. God won't leave you to fend for yourself. He loves you too much."

A Way to Escape

With that settled, Stephanie brightened. Looking out the window, she suddenly became aware of her surroundings.

"Hey, Skip, where are we going?"

"We're going to visit Cassandra's aunt and uncle. They live on a big ranch. You'll love the wide open space."

"Why didn't Cassandra come with you to get me?"

"She wasn't there when I left. She took off early this morning to go help feed the animals on a farm and hadn't returned yet."

Skip turned onto the private property and drove past the 'No Trespassing' sign. A moment later, he parked the car in front of the house.

Stephanie threw open her car door and leaped out. "Come on, Skip." She raced around and yanked open his door.

Skip slid off the seat with a grin. He stepped around to the trunk of the car and retrieved Stephanie's suitcase. Then he took her hand and escorted her up the porch steps into the ranch house. Mabel came bustling from the kitchen, talking as she wiped her hands on her apron.

"Well, it's about time ... Oh, Skip. I'm sorry. I thought you were Woody."

"Was he supposed to be back by now?"

"I expected him home for lunch an hour ago." She glanced at the corner grandfather clock. "I don't understand what's keeping him. Woody's never been this late before. I sent Dale and Cassandra out looking for him, but they haven't returned yet, either."

"How long ago was that?"

"About twenty minutes, and I'm getting concerned."

"Aunt Mabel, this is my sister, Stephanie."

"Oh, you're a pretty little thing." Mabel reached for her suitcase, and Skip handed it to her.

Stephanie blushed and ducked behind Skip.

"Do you want me to go look for Dale and Cassandra?" asked Skip.

Mabel shook her head. "No, dear. You'd have to go by horseback and you could get lost. This property is massive. We'll give them until two o'clock. That's another forty minutes. If they're not back by then, something is definitely wrong. Now, Stephanie, I have just the room for you. Let's get you settled. Then we'll come get something cold to drink while we're waiting for Dale and Cassandra. Okay?"

Stephanie popped her head out from behind her brother and nodded.

"Good. Come with me." Aunt Mabel held out her hand to Stephanie.

Stephanie grasped Mabel's hand, and Skip trailed them down the hall to a pretty pink bedroom with a full-sized canopy bed.

"This is where I'm sleeping?" gasped Stephanie. "Oh, I like it."

It took Mabel less than five minutes to empty Stephanie's suitcase into the drawer.

Then Mabel led them back to the kitchen. "How about some ice cold lemonade?" She set the pitcher on the table.

"Yum, I love lemonade," said Stephanie. "But Skip doesn't like it."

"That's quite all right," said Mabel, pulling out another pitcher. "Because neither does Dale. But we also have ice tea."

They had barely sat down with their drinks when the door burst open. Cassandra and Dale raced into the kitchen.

"Aunt Mabel, the ranch hands haven't seen Uncle Woody today," said Cassandra. "Dale and I looked everywhere we thought he might be."

"Maybe he went into town," said Skip.

"I suppose that's possible," said Mabel. "I'll call Sheriff Robins and see if he's seen Woody today."

While Mabel stepped away to make the call, Cassandra and Dale helped themselves to cold drinks.

"Stephanie, what are you doing here?" asked Cassandra.

Without waiting for her response, Dale and Cassandra lowered their voices and turned to Skip.

"Something funny is going on at the farm," said Cassandra.

Dale nodded. "Half the animals had been fed by the time we got there."

"It looked like someone had interrupted whoever was taking care of them. Dale and I finished feeding them, milked the cows, collected the eggs, and did the chores."

"Plus, there was a stack of dirty dishes in the sink," said Dale. "When we left yesterday, the only dishes we'd left were the glasses that we'd been drinking out of. Remember?"

Skip nodded.

"It's spooky," said Cassandra.

Stephanie shuddered.

"Sounds to me as if someone has taken up residence," said Skip. "Why don't we head out there and look around."

"Can I go?" asked Stephanie.

"Sure," said Skip.

Mabel hung up the phone and returned to the table. "The sheriff hasn't seen Woody today, but he'll check around town for me."

"Aunt Mabel, we're going to take Stephanie out to the farm," said Cassandra. "We'll watch for Uncle Woody."

"Thank you, dear. I appreciate it."

"Let's pray before we go," suggested Skip.

All heads bowed.

Skip spoke softly. "Heavenly Father, thank You for guiding and protecting us daily. Please protect Woody, wherever he is, and bring him home safely. If he needs help, lead us to him. Bless Aunt Mabel with Your peace and help her to trust You to care for her husband. In Jesus' name. Amen."

Skip trailed the others as they neared the stable. He wasn't in a hurry to get back on a horse. Why couldn't they just take the car?

Cassandra slid her arm around him. "You all right?"

Dale dashed ahead of them. "Come on, Stephanie. Help me get the horses ready."

"Okay" Stephanie raced after him.

Taking Skip's hand in hers, Cassandra slowed her pace. "Why don't we have Dale saddle Cupcake for you again? I mean, we're not in any hurry to get there."

"You really don't mind?"

"No. You take the time you need to get comfortable riding."

"Thanks, Cassie. That means a lot to me."

Sliding her arms around his neck, Cassandra pulled him into a kiss. "You are adorable." She kissed him again.

Holding hands, Skip and Cassandra strolled into the barn. Dale was fastening the saddle on Cupcake while Stephanie stroked and petted the other two horses, which were already saddled and ready to go.

"Come on, Stephie," called Cassandra. "You ride with me."

Cassandra mounted Lightning and grasped Stephanie's hand, pulling her up into the saddle. Dale mounted his horse, and Skip climbed into the saddle the way he'd seen Dale and Cassandra do it.

Dale led the way, nudging his horse into a trot, but Cassandra hung back to ride slowly with Skip. Beginning to feel comfortable on Cupcake, Skip decided to allow her to trot, so he urged his horse after Dale, and Cassandra rode beside him.

Rusty anxiously paced the basement floor of the Benson's farmhouse. After those two kids left, he dragged that young woman upstairs to fix them a bite to eat and clean up the kitchen. She might come in handy to have around.

"Not bad." Rusty licked his fingers and turned to Kyle. "Now, aren't you glad I grabbed her?"

"No. I would have been happier if we could have pulled this off without any hostages, not even Woody. But he had the key we needed to get in. I understood why we had to grab him."

"I told you, Kyle. She came looking for that money, and she wasn't going to leave until she found it. What did you want me to do? Stay hidden until she got tired and left in a month or two or help her find it, and hand it over to her."

"Okay. Okay."

"I promise – no more hostages. Now let's start hauling some of this good stuff out of here."

"And what if those two kids come back?"

"They have no reason to come back today. All the animals have been taken care of. The chores are done. Trust me. They won't be back."

"Okay," said Kyle. "That makes sense. We need to organize and inventory this stuff before we carry it upstairs. That way, we'll know what we got."

It didn't take them nearly as long to reach the farm today as it seemed to yesterday, but Skip allowed Cupcake to trot most of the way. Reaching the farm, they investigated the grounds near the house and barn before dismounting.

"Everything looks the way we left it," said Cassandra.

"Let's go in the house and look around," said Dale.

Skip dismounted and reached up to help his little sister.

Stephanie smiled when he lifted her down. "Thanks, Skip."

Taking his hand, Cassandra hopped to the ground. "You are such a gentleman." She cupped his face in her hands and kissed him. "I love it, and I love you."

Skip grinned.

Dale led the horses into the barn where they could rest.

Stephanie followed. "Wow! This is neat! How do you get up there?" She pointed at the loft.

Dale chuckled. "A ladder, silly. And you get down the same way, unless you're like me. I swing down like Tarzan."

"Can I go up there?"

"Sure. Come on."

While Dale and Stephanie climbed to the loft, Skip and Cassandra looked over the rest of the barn. Skip didn't know what he was looking for, but he looked anyway.

"Anything unusual up there?" he asked Dale.

"Nope. Everything is exactly as I left it yesterday. How about down there?"

"I wouldn't know, but everything looks okay. Let's go check the house."

Dale grabbed the rope and swung down like Tarzan so Stephanie could see how it was done.

"Can I try it?"

"No. You use the ladder," said Skip.

Stephanie frowned, but obeyed. As soon as her feet touched the ground, she dashed out the barn door, racing to the house. Dale, Cassandra, and Skip ambled after her. When they reached the house, she was nowhere around.

"Stephanie!" called Skip.

Dale unlocked the front door while Cassandra ran around to check the back. The boys entered through the front and met Cassandra in the living room.

"The back door was open. Stephanie must be in the house."

Skip looked toward the kitchen. "Oo, something smells good."

"Mm, yeah." Dale drifted toward the kitchen, but Skip grabbed his arm.

"See if you can find Stephanie."

While Dale searched for Stephanie, Skip and Cassandra separated, looking through the first floor of the large farmhouse.

"Skip."

Skip hurried into the kitchen.

"The sink's empty." Cassandra looked from the sink to Skip in bewilderment. "Where are the dishes?"

Skip pursed his lips and raised an eyebrow. He unlocked the dishwasher and opened it up. There they were.

"Well, they're clean," he said.

"How do you know that?"

"Feel them. Everything's still hot. The dishwasher was just run."

"Skip, do you believe in ghosts?"

Skip burst into laughter. "No. I suspect there's someone else here. Someone who eats. Ghosts don't eat."

Just then, Stephanie screamed.

Chapter 28

The Mysterious Voices

Rusty stormed back and forth, his fists clenched, ready to pound someone. "I can't take any more of this, Kyle. Yesterday, Doug was arrested. We have two hostages we don't want."

"Shh, Rusty, lower your voice."

"We can't find that money. Every time we start to unload this basement full of electronics, someone walks in on us. Now we've got a houseful of kids."

"Rusty, will you shut up. All you do is complain."

"How are we supposed to get out of here with those kids here?" yelled Rusty.

"I don't know, but lower your voice."

"We're going to have to take them *all* hostage."

"Are you crazy?" cried Kyle.

"It's the only way."

"No, Rusty. *No more hostages.*"

Abandoning their investigation, Skip and Cassandra raced into the living room, nearly colliding with Dale who dashed in from another direction. Pale and trembling, Stephanie sped through another doorway into Skip's arms.

"Hey, what happened?" asked Skip. "Stephanie?"

Stephanie paused, listening. "Well, I ... I heard ... I mean, I know what I heard. Didn't anybody else hear it?"

The other three exchanged glances.

"Hear what?" asked Cassandra. "What did you hear?"

"Voices. They weren't your voices. They were fighting."

"What did they say?" asked Skip.

"I don't know. It sounded like it was far away. I got scared and screamed."

"Show us where you heard them," said Skip. Cassandra and the boys followed Stephanie back to a bedroom.

"This is Doug's room," said Dale.

"Shh." Skip put his finger to his lips and everyone listened.

"I don't hear anything," said Cassandra. "Stephanie, are you sure you didn't hear us?"

"Were you and Skip fighting?"

"No."

"Then I'm sure it wasn't you."

Everyone listened again. The silence was deafening.

Skip lowered his voice to a whisper. "Someone is in this house besides us. Cassandra, maybe it would be safer for you and Stephanie to wait for us outside. Jump on your horse and take her for a ride around the yard. Dale and I are going to search this house."

"Okay. Come on, Stephie."

"Cassie, if anything happens, don't come looking for us. Ride into town and get the sheriff."

Cassandra nodded and grasped Stephanie's hand, escorting her out the door.

"Come on, Dale. I want to search every last room."

The old farmhouse was extensive from many additions. The boys climbed the stairs to the second floor and began their search, opening every door and exploring any possible hideout. Finding nothing, they crept silently back down the stairs to inspect the lower floor. At the end of the hallway was a door. Skip gripped the knob, but it was locked.

"Hey, Dale, you got a key for this door?"

"No, I sure don't."

"What's in here?"

Dale shrugged. "That's Doug's library. He never allowed me in there."

"Why not? If it's just a library, what's the big deal?"

"Doug collected rare and priceless books. One time, I accidentally returned one of his books to the public library. It took us weeks to run it down and get it back."

"Oh." Skip glanced at his wristwatch. "It's getting late. Go call Aunt Mabel to see if Woody has returned home yet."

"Good idea."

Dale hurried into the kitchen while Skip checked the rest of the first-floor rooms.

Pushing through the kitchen door, Dale met Skip in the living room. "I talked to Aunt Mabel. He hasn't come home, yet."

"And I didn't find any sign of anyone in here. Come on. Let's go look for Woody."

The boys left the house and locked the door behind them. Racing to the barn, Dale mounted up and led Skip's horse to him.

"Find anything?" Cassandra galloped over to them on Lightning. Stephanie sat in front of her.

Skip shook his head. "No." He climbed into the saddle and directed Cupcake toward home. "We just called your Aunt Mabel. It's almost supper time, but Uncle Woody still hasn't returned. Any ideas where else we could look, Cassandra?"

"We already checked the obvious places."

With Dale and Cassandra riding on either side of Skip, the horses plodded toward home.

Skip rubbed his chin, thinking aloud. "When Woody left this morning, he was headed up to the north end of the ranch, but he never got there."

"No, he wasn't," said Dale. "Uncle Woody ran over to the farm to do an inventory of things that needed taken care of before putting the place up for sale. I gave him Doug's keys so he could get into the house."

"Then we need to search the farmland and the trails leading back to the ranch," said Skip.

By the time the foursome reached home, it was well past mealtime, and they were famished. The girls entered the house while Skip helped Dale unsaddle the horses and set them free inside the corral.

"After supper, we'll round up fresh horses," said Dale.

Skip cringed at the thought of riding a different horse. He'd just gotten used to Cupcake. But Dale would laugh at him if he found out about his fear of horses. And since Woody wasn't there to run interference for him, he'd have to collect the courage to climb onto a strange horse.

Sliding his hands into his pockets, he strolled toward the house beside Dale, baffled by Woody's sudden disappearance. The boys entered the house and washed up. Dale plunked down on his chair, but Skip seated the girls first. He waited patiently for Aunt Mabel to join them so he could seat her as well.

"Aunt Mabel, are you going to eat with us?" he asked.

"No." Tears trailing down her cheeks, Mabel dashed from the dining room.

Skip winced when a door slammed down the hall. "You guys pray and eat. I'll be right back." Hurrying after her, he paused outside her bedroom door.

"Aunt Mabel?" Skip knocked softly. When she didn't answer, he turned the knob and peeked into the room.

Mabel sat on the bed crying.

Skip sat down beside her, comforting her with a hug. "We'll find him."

"But will we find him alive? Oh, Skip, I'm so scared."

"Woody is in God's hands, Aunt Mabel. Now, you come eat while I call the sheriff. After we eat, we'll go look for him again. We're not giving up."

Aunt Mabel smiled through her tears. "Thank you for giving me hope."

"Our hope is in the Lord." With a reassuring smile, he escorted Mabel back to the dining room and seated her at the table before calling the sheriff. A moment later, he rejoined the others.

"What did the sheriff say?" asked Mabel.

"He said that no one in town has seen him, but he's asked folks to be on the look-out for him. And he'll check with some of your nearest neighbors, so don't worry. Surely, someone has seen him. After we eat, we'll ride back out to the Benson farm. Something strange is going on out there. That's where Woody was headed when he disappeared, and I'm wondering if somehow the two are related."

Chapter 29

New Developments

Skip cleared and wiped the table while Dale and Cassandra put up the leftover food and loaded the dishwasher.

"Come on, Skip, let's go," said Stephanie.

Dale and Skip exchanged glances.

"Um, Stephanie, I think it would be safer if you stayed here," said Skip.

"I want to go."

"I know, but Aunt Mabel really needs some company right now."

Stephanie glanced over at Mabel's tear-filled eyes, and all arguments died in her throat. "All right. Can I go next time?"

"Maybe next time."

A Way to Escape

In the remaining daylight, Cassandra and the boys rounded up three fresh horses and saddled them. Seeing his riding companions mount up, Skip climbed into the saddle, and they started down the trail toward the Benson farm. As they rode, they watched for any signs of Woody.

Skip noticed that Dale and Cassandra's horses were spirited, whereas his was mellow, like Cupcake. He was starting to enjoy these rides.

With a grin, Cassandra blew him a kiss. Skip smiled. She picked out a horse with an easy-going temperament for him.

"Skip, anytime you feel ready for the challenge, let us know, and we'll pick up our pace a little," said Dale.

Glancing from Cassandra to Dale, he realized that he was once again riding in the middle. These two were watching out for him.

"Thanks, Dale. I think I'm ready now. I'm definitely anxious to get back out to the farm."

"Then let's go." Dale nudged his horse into a trot.

Skip found it enjoyable to pick up a little speed.

"Boy, I thought those kids would never leave this afternoon." Rusty maneuvered the red pickup truck back into the farmhouse garage.

Climbing out of the truck, Kyle sighed. "Me, too. Well, at least we got a few things out of the house. While we have an opportunity, let's search Doug's library for that money."

Trotting toward the house, Kyle let them in and relocked the front door before hustling down the hall to the library."

"Doug intended to deposit it in the bank, so I think we're wasting our time looking for it," said Rusty.

Unlocking the library door, Kyle shook his head. "He got arrested yesterday afternoon. I don't think he had time to get to the bank."

Arriving at the farm, the boys hitched the horses near the barn and escorted Cassandra across the yard to the house. Skip squatted close to the ground, examining tire tracks.

"Dale, come look at this."

A few long strides brought Dale to Skip's side.

"I don't remember these truck tire tracks being here earlier."

Dale knelt down to examine the ground. "They look fresh. Doug has a red pick-up, but it's in the garage."

"Interesting. Let's go see if there are any new developments in the house."

Cassandra and the boys entered the front door quietly. Everything looked just like they had left it, except ...

"Dale, the library door is open," said Skip. "Someone has definitely been in this house. They may still be here."

"That's impossible. Everything was locked up when we left," said Dale.

"Then whoever's here has a key, because last time we found the back door unlocked and the library door locked."

Dale thought for a moment. "But there are only two sets of keys. I have one, and Uncle Woody has the other. Come to think of it, I gave him Doug's keys, and I think Doug's set of keys had his truck key on the ring and the key to the library."

"Then Uncle Woody might be here somewhere."

"Oh, Skip, don't be ridiculous," said Cassandra. "My uncle wouldn't be involved in any pranks like this, especially when Aunt Mabel would worry about him not coming home."

"Come on," said Skip. "I want to search the library while the door is open."

Dale and Cassandra followed him through the doorway. The room was lined with books. An easy chair sat in the corner, a small desk beside it. Skip pulled the chair away from the wall and rummaged through the desk. He pulled books from the bookcases, searching the shelves and thumbing through the books.

"What are you doing?" asked Dale.

"Looking for any secret device." Skip opened a large, thick hardback book and gasped. It was actually a box, loaded with money.

"Wow!" cried Dale.

"I think it's time to get the sheriff involved in this," said Skip.

A door slammed down the hall, and all three jumped. Shoving the box into Dale's hands, Skip yanked out his 9 mm Glock and raced down the hall. Crouching low, his gun ready, he searched the downstairs rooms. Cassandra and Dale hurried after him.

"I guess he got away." Skip re-holstered his gun. Had he been alone, he wouldn't have given up the search so quickly, but he didn't want to inadvertently lead Cassandra or Dale into danger.

Cassandra swallowed hard and looped her arm through his, clinging to him. "S-Skip, let's go home. It's long since dark, and I'm scared."

"Okay." Skip took the box of money from Dale. "Lock up, Dale. Let's go home."

With a grin, Dale hurriedly obeyed. The three made their way through the dark to the barn and rounded up their horses. Anxious to get home, they let their horses follow the dark trail to the bucket of oats that rewarded nearly every ride.

Discouraged and weary, Cassandra and the boys softly entered the house. Aunt Mabel peeked out of the kitchen, her face red from crying.

"I'm so sorry, Aunt Mabel," said Skip. "Let's pray for Woody again."

Gathering around Aunt Mabel, Skip held the box under his arm and prayed for Woody, asking God to send angels to protect him and bring him home safely.

Aunt Mabel wiped her eyes and hugged Skip. "You're a fine boy, Skip. What's in the box?"

"Cash. We found it tonight. May I use the phone to call the sheriff?"

"Absolutely. His number is posted by the phone."

Skip stepped into the kitchen and punched in the sheriff's number.

"Sheriff Robins."

"Sheriff, this is Skip. I'm sorry to call so late, but there's something strange going on at the Benson farm. Strange noises. Doors slamming."

"Sounds like someone's in the house. I'll check it out tomorrow."

"One more thing. This evening we found a box full of cash."

"Put it in a safe place, and I'll stop by Woody's ranch tomorrow to talk to you about it. I think I know who that belongs to."

"Yes, sir."

"And thanks for calling, Skip. I'll see you tomorrow."

Skip hung up and joined the others in the living room.

"Well, it's getting late," said Mabel. "You kids better hit the sack. Skip, you need to kiss Stephanie good night. I promised her you would."

"Okay." Skip kissed Cassandra and whispered in her ear. "Go get ready for bed. I'll be right there."

The instant Cassandra dashed off, Skip grabbed Dale's arm and pulled the boy close to him, lowering his voice. "Meet me outside at midnight. We're spending the night at your farm."

Dale nodded. Slipping down the hallway, he disappeared into his room.

Chapter 30

Stake Out

Crawling out of Doug's closet, Rusty heaved a sigh. "Can you believe this luck we're having?"

"They almost spotted us," said Kyle. "I barely got out of the library before they saw me."

"Hey, I just wanted to grab a bite to eat in the kitchen. I'm hungry."

"Come to think of it, I am, too."

"Well, they're not coming back tonight," said Rusty.

"That's what you said last time."

"It's after eleven, Kyle. Do you expect them to come back tonight?"

"No, I really don't. But I wouldn't be at all surprised if they showed up by sunrise."

"So, then, we have to get everything done tonight."

Kyle nodded. "And be out of here by first light."

"Well, I'm hungry. Let's eat first."

Glancing over at the open library door, Kyle nodded. "I'm for that. We'll eat down in the basement because I want to feed our hostages. The last time they ate was this morning, and it might be two or three days before anyone finds them."

"If you insist."

"I do," said Kyle. "After we eat, we'll search the library for that money. Then we'll load Doug's truck with as much valuable electronics as we can haul, which should be most of it, and we'll be gone before those kids even wake up tomorrow morning."

"I like it." Rusty hastened into the kitchen and pulled out a frying pan while Kyle yanked the bacon from the refrigerator drawer.

Shortly before midnight, Skip crawled out of bed and slipped into clean clothes. He scribbled a note to his sleeping wife, grabbed his car keys, and crept silently out the door. Trotting around to the front of the house, he met Dale.

"I got the horses ready," said Dale, speaking softly.

"Horses?" echoed Skip. "Oh, that's right. I grabbed my car keys out of habit."

"Habits are hard to break, aren't they? Let's go."

Skip smiled when he saw Cupcake waiting for him tied to the corral fence. Quietly mounting up, the boys headed for the Benson farm. Pondering on the importance of leaving silently and arriving at the farm just as quietly so as not to alert others of their presence, Skip now appreciated the benefit of riding a horse. A car would make too much noise.

"There was an awful lot of hundred dollar bills in that box," said Dale. "Do you think Doug stole it?"

"That's my guess. Cassandra and I counted over a hundred thousand dollars."

Dale whistled.

The light from a full moon guided them all the way to the farm. Dismounting, the boys tethered the horses and silently entered the house.

"Maybe we can catch the culprits when they make their move," said Skip.

"You think they'll try something tonight?"

"Possibly. They can't do anything during the day when there are so many people coming in and out."

Dale nodded. "Where shall we set up our stake-out?"

"Let's see if the library is still open. I have a feeling that's our focal point."

Dale led the way down the long, dark hallway. The door was still open, so the boys sat down in a corner of the dark room to wait and watch.

"Let's pray for Woody again," said Skip.

"It won't do any good. Everyone knows that there's no God."

"Of course, there's a God. And He answers prayer."

"How do you know that?" asked Dale.

"Because I'm a product of answered prayer."

"How?"

"It's a long story."

"So tell it. We have all night."

Skip sprawled out on the floor and propped his head on his hand. "Well, when I was a kid, I wanted to be a baseball star. I thought of nothing else."

Dale's eyes widened with interest.

"The older I got, the more I resented my parents for telling me what to do. I thought that baseball stars didn't have to do dumb things like make their beds or watch their baby sister."

"So what happened?"

"I was raised in church. My mom and dad were both Christians, and I had accepted the Lord as my Savior when I was seven. But the older I got, the more I did what I wanted to do, and responsibility wasn't on my agenda."

Skip heaved a sigh. "I knew deep down in my heart that I was disobeying everything that God wanted me to do, but I wasn't ready to surrender my will. I stopped praying. I stopped reading my Bible. I tried to skip church, but my parents wouldn't let me. And I resisted their discipline and authority."

Dale shifted positions. "What did they do?"

"My parents started praying for me harder than they had ever prayed for anything in their lives. They had prayed for me before, but this was a different kind of praying. My dad was a mighty man of prayer. He prayed that God would do whatever was necessary to teach me responsibility and draw me close."

"Did He?" asked Dale.

With tears trickling down his cheeks, Skip nodded. "The very next day, my father was killed."

Dale gasped. "You're kidding! How?"

"My dad was a police officer. We stopped at a mini market on our way home from baseball practice, and he ran inside to grab me a soda. At that exact moment, the store was being robbed, and the thief blasted my father with a shotgun."

"How horrible," cried Dale.

"Shh." Skip lowered his voice. "You know what's ironic about it? I married the killer's daughter."

Dale blinked a couple times and stared at Skip in disbelief. "You did what?" Without waiting for a response, he said, "Now everything makes sense. We knew that Cassandra's dad was in prison for armed robbery, but we didn't have the whole story."

"Well, now you have it."

"Skip, do you think that God's responsible for your father's death?"

"I believe He allowed it to get my attention. Boy, He got it in a hurry. I still wonder how different my life might be if I hadn't been rebellious. I might be a ballplayer today instead of a Forest Valley police officer."

"Doug always said there is no God."

"What do you think, Dale?"

"I ... I don't know any more."

"Let's pray for Woody. And you, too, okay?"

"Okay."

A Way to Escape

Rolling to his stomach, Skip folded his hands and bowed his head, praying earnestly that God would protect Woody and reveal Himself to Dale. By the time he finished, they were both rubbing their eyes and yawning.

The last thing Skip heard was the four consecutive chimes of the library clock.

Stomping back and forth in the basement, Rusty slammed his right fist into the palm of his left hand. "We are *never* going to find that money and get this stuff out of here."

Kyle looked toward the ceiling and heaved a frustrated sigh. "I know. I think at this point, we just need to get out of here."

"How? Those boys are upstairs in the library."

"Probably asleep. We've been waiting for them to leave for hours. It's now daylight, and we have to get out of here before this place is crawling with activity. I'll go find out what those kids are doing. If I can slip by them without being seen, I'll head outside. I'll cut the phone lines, so if we should accidentally wake them, they won't be able to phone for help. Give me ten minutes, then follow me out. I'll meet you in the garage."

"And leave all this good stuff behind?"

"Rusty, didn't you say that boy's a cop? Don't you suppose by now he's alerted the sheriff?"

"Good point. I just hate the thought of leaving all these valuable things behind. Just think how much money it could bring us."

"Not a dime if we get caught. Now, I'll wait for you at the truck. Give me at least a five-minute head start. While you're waiting, if you want to sort through the small stuff and pocket a few easy-to-carry items, that's fine, but nothing heavy or difficult to carry." Kyle spun on his heel and headed toward the ladder.

Rusty glared after him. Kyle was always telling him what to do. He wasn't the boss. Doug was. And with Doug gone, he no longer answered to anybody. He would do what he wanted, and he wasn't certain that he wanted to abandon all this good, salable merchandise.

Chapter 31

Another Disappearance

Awakened from a sound sleep, Skip bolted upright. What was that noise? Did he hear it or did he dream it? His eyes darted around the sunlit room as light streamed through the thin curtains that covered the corner windows. Dale lay near him sound asleep.

Leaping up, Skip pulled out his gun and crept through the silent house searching for unwelcome visitors, but once again his search turned up empty. Returning to the library, he shook Dale awake.

"Hm?" Dale slowly sat up, yawning and rubbing his eyes. "What's the matter?"

"Did you hear that noise?"

Dale shook his head and started to lay back down.

"Someone's in this house besides us. We'd better check on the horses, and make sure someone didn't turn them loose."

"Okay." Stumbling to his feet, Dale staggered after Skip.

The boys left the house and hiked down the trail to the barn where they'd left the horses. Both horses were still in their stalls.

Dale yawned. "What time is it?"

Skip glanced at his wristwatch. "A little after seven."

The clip-clop of horses hooves rapidly approached the barn, and Cassandra rode up. "Hi, fellows. Sleep well?"

Skip chuckled. "What do you think? And how did you manage to sneak off without Stephanie?"

"I didn't. She came with me."

"Then where is she?

"I dropped her off at the house to run in and get a drink of water."

"By herself?" Skip bolted from the barn. *"Stephanie!"* Filled with intense fear, he dashed into the house. "Stephanie, where are you?"

As Dale caught up with him, they separated, running through the house calling her name. After a thorough search, the boys met Cassandra in the living room.

"Okay, mustn't panic." Skip dropped onto the sofa and buried his face in his hands. With a sigh, he looked up again. "Cassandra, did you actually see her enter the house?"

"No. I let her off the horse and took off to find you guys. Oh, Skip. I'm so sorry." Tears pooled in Cassandra's eyes, and she knelt in front of him.

"Dale, go search outside," said Skip. "Look any place a child could hide or might want to play. Cassandra and I will search the house again."

Dale nodded solemnly and dashed outside.

"We'll look around again. Stephanie has to be here somewhere." Skip took Cassandra's hand and led her down the hallway. "Stephanie! Stephanie, where are you?"

A muffled crash halted their steps.

"What was that?" said Cassandra.

The two stood still, listening intently, but no other sound followed. Skip glanced around. "And where did it come from?"

Combing the interior once more proved fruitless for Skip and Cassandra. No Stephanie. No clues as to what caused the mysterious noise.

"I don't get it," said Cassandra. "Stephanie just disappeared. And I know we heard a crash. Where's the mess?"

"That's a good question." Skip stepped outside, glancing around. "Now, where did Dale go?" Cupping his hands to his mouth, he yelled. "Dale!"

No answer.

"Dale!" hollered Cassandra. "Where are you? *Dale!*"

"Now where could he have gone?" Skip slid his hands into his pockets and trotted toward the barn. "Dale? Are you in here?"

Dashing after him, Cassandra looped her arm through his. "Skip, I'm scared. Let's get out of here."

"We can't, Cassandra. We can't leave without Dale and Stephanie. You wait here. I'm climbing up to the loft to look around."

"I'm not staying here by myself."

Skip sighed. "Okay. Then you go first. I'll be right behind you."

Releasing his arm, Cassandra started up the ladder. Skip followed, but found the barn loft as empty as the house.

"They've vanished," said Cassandra. "This place is haunted."

Skip climbed back down the ladder and led her out the barn door. "Come on, Cassandra. You don't really believe that, do you?"

"Don't you?"

"No. There is an explanation. I just wish I knew what it was."

"Well, right now, I don't care what it is. I just want to get out of here before *we* disappear."

"That's a good idea. You ride into town and get the sheriff."

"B-b-by myself?"

"Sure, you'll be safe. Everything that's happened has occurred on this property."

"What if you disappear while I'm gone?"

"I won't."

"But what if you do?"

Skip grasped her arms. "Cassandra, I'm not leaving here without Dale and Stephanie. Do you understand?"

Cassandra nodded. "I want to stay with you. Maybe we can call the sheriff on the telephone."

"We can do that." Holding hands, Skip and Cassandra hurried across the yard into the house.

Cassandra snatched up the receiver and the color left her cheeks. "The phone is dead."

"Then you'll have to ride into town."

"I can't, Skip. I'm scared. I'm afraid that you'll disappear while I'm gone. Please, let's go together."

Skip shook his head. "No, Cassandra. I'm not leaving. You have to go."

"Isn't there any other way?" Tears spilled down her cheeks.

"Afraid not." Grasping her hand, Skip led her back to the barn. "I'll be okay. I promise. Now, the sooner you leave, the sooner you'll be able to round up help."

"You'd better be here when I get back."

Skip cupped her chin and kissed her. "I will be. Now, get going."

Scrambling into Lightning's saddle, Cassandra wheeled the horse and galloped off. Skip watched until she was out of sight. Spinning around, he shaded his eyes with his hand as he scanned the yard.

"Hm. I haven't checked the pigpen or the chicken coop or the ..." He raised an eyebrow. "... the garage."

Entering through the side door, Skip glanced around. "Dale? Stephanie? Woody?"

A Way to Escape

The over-sized garage housed a big red pick-up truck, tractor, and farm equipment. Skip paused to examine the truck tires. They were caked with soft dirt.

"This thing's been driven recently." Cupping his hands to his mouth, he called out, "Anybody in here?" His eyes scanned the dimly-lit garage. "Stephanie? Dale?"

"Skip?" came a muffled reply.

Skip paused, listening. "Dale?"

"Get me out of here!"

He heard pounding coming from a storage closet.

Skip scrambled over equipment to reach the metal door. "Dale, are you in there?"

"I'm locked in. Get me out of here."

Skip yanked a sticky note off the door before turning the key, which was still in the lock. He slowly opened the door.

"Are you all right? What happened?"

"I stepped inside to look for Stephanie. Someone shoved me in and locked the door."

"Did you get a look at them?"

Dale shook his head. "Not even a glimpse. What do you got?"

"A note. It was on the outside of the door."

"What's it say?"

"Leave while there's still time."

Chapter 32

An Escape Attempt

Peeking from around the side of the garage, Kyle saw Skip send the girl away. Standing outside the barn, the boy watched her ride off before turning and heading for the garage. The moment he disappeared inside, Kyle dashed back to the house to see what had become of his idiotic partner. Rusty was supposed to meet him at the truck *before* Doug's kid brother wandered in.

Kyle hustled inside and dashed down the hallway, ducking into Doug's room. He yanked open the closet door and lifted a trap door. As he descended the ladder, he pulled the trap door closed behind him. Once his feet touched the floor, he spun around in anger, ready to explode all over Rusty, only to find him wrestling with a little girl.

He'd taped her mouth shut to keep her quiet and fought to hold her still as he tied her wrists together behind her back. A shattered television set covered the floor.

Great. Now they had *three* hostages. And one of them was a child no older than nine or ten years old. Kyle wanted to beat some sense into his irrational partner, but it was a little late for that.

Rusty struggled with the hysterical child, who was crying and kicking when he seized her arm and jerked her to her feet. Dragging her across the room, he shoved her down and stormed away. The girl tumbled to the concrete beside their other two hostages.

"Rusty, I thought we agreed that we'd take no more hostages."

"Well, I didn't intend to grab her. I followed you upstairs exactly ten minutes later like you told me to. The boys were gone, and I saw the girl ride past the house on the horse, so to be safe, I decided to slip out the back door so they didn't see me. When I was sneaking through the living room, I caught sight of that little girl coming from the kitchen, and she saw me at the same time. She screamed, and I grabbed her and slapped my hand over her mouth to keep her quiet. What else could I have done, Kyle?"

Kyle sighed.

"If I had just run, she would have taken off outside screaming and alerted those other kids, and believe me, I didn't want another encounter with Skip. And once I grabbed her and shut her up, I couldn't just let her go, now could I?"

"No, I guess not. I got cornered in the garage while waiting for you. Doug's kid brother wandered in looking for *her*."

Kyle pointed at the little girl. "Of course, he didn't know I was in there. When he wasn't looking, I shoved him from behind into a storage closet and locked him in. Then I slapped a note on the door, hoping it would scare those kids enough to get them to leave long enough for us to escape."

With a sigh, Kyle continued. "Unfortunately, holding onto this child creates quite a dilemma for us. Those kids don't know about that one."

He pointed to the young woman. "And they only suspect that Woody's disappearance is related. But with *her* missing ..." Kyle pointed to the little girl. "... Cassandra will return with the sheriff and half the town to tear this place apart in order to find her. And we'll *never* get out of here."

Chapter 33

Unanswered Questions

Skip handed Dale the small paper.

"While there's still time?" Dale studied the cryptic note. "While there's still time for what?"

"To leave, I suppose. But I'm not leaving without my sister."

"Where's Cassandra?"

"I sent her for the sheriff."

"Why didn't you just call him?"

"The phone's dead," said Skip. "The wires were cut."

Dale raised an eyebrow. "Maybe we should stay together from now on."

"I was thinking the same thing. By the way, I found the source of those fresh tire tracks." Skip patted the hood of the red pick-up truck. "Right here."

"That's not possible. This is Doug's truck. No one else drives it."

"Well, someone did. Check the tires. They're caked with soft dirt. Someone drove this truck quite recently." Skip started toward the door. "Come on. We have to find Stephanie. Dale, you've lived here your whole life. Does that old house have any secret tunnels or trap doors?"

"Not that I know of. Why?"

"Awhile ago, Cassandra and I heard a crash inside the house. We went through every room and found no evidence of anything that could have caused that noise."

Dale shrugged. "I don't know. Doug was always very secretive." Climbing over the clutter in the garage, the boys made their way outside. The cows were bawling loudly. "Hey, Skip, what time is it?"

Skip glanced at his watch. "Ten thirty. Why? Are you hungry?"

"Yes, but I haven't fed the animals yet or milked the cows. I know we have to find Stephanie, but the chores need done, too."

With a sigh, Skip crammed his hands in his pockets and grasped his keys. "I know."

Unfamiliar with farm chores, Skip mostly watched while Dale took care of the animals. Skip followed him around the farm while he went from one chore to another. When he finally finished taking care of the animals, he once again asked Skip the time.

"Almost twelve thirty." Skip yawned. A warm breeze ruffled his hair. Folding his arms on the corral fence, he rested his head on them and closed his eyes. Dread washed over him as he wondered what had become of his little sister.

"Nice day, isn't it?" said Dale.

Skip blinked back tears and swallowed hard. *Not for Stephanie.*

"Skip?"

Or me, either, for that matter. First Woody. Now Stephanie. And I'm scared. He wasn't scared for himself. He feared that he might never see them alive again.

"I'm finished with the chores," said Dale. "Shouldn't Cassandra be back by now?"

"I would have thought so."

"I hope she didn't run into any problems."

Skip looked at him. "Me, too."

Dale climbed onto the fence and sat down, watching the horses graze. Skip once again dropped his head into his folded arms.

When Cassandra and Mabel arrived at the farmhouse, the boys stood quite some distance away at the corral fence. Neither of them turned when the car pulled up beside the house.

Cassandra heaved a sigh of relief and slid from the car. "There's Dale."

With a smile, Mabel also stepped from the vehicle. "And Skip, too. See? He didn't disappear. But the sheriff's not here yet."

"Sheriff Robins said he'd round up a search party first. He should be here soon." Cassandra's heart went out to Skip. "Poor Skip. Aunt Mabel, I feel awful. I can't believe I was so careless."

"Go see him, Cassandra. I'll get lunch on the table. I'll bet they haven't eaten yet."

Opening the back car door, Mabel pulled out a picnic basket. Cassandra held the door for her. Then she trotted over to the boys. Sliding her arm around Skip, she kissed his cheek.

"Angel, are you hungry? We brought lunch."

"Lunch." Dale bounded off the fence and raced to the house.

Skip raised his head and looked at her. "Thanks, Cassandra, but I can't eat right now."

"Skip, I'm so sorry. Don't worry. We'll find Stephanie. The sheriff said he'd be over as soon as he rounded up a search party."

"I fear her life may be in great danger, if she's even still alive. See what I found?"

Cassandra took the paper from his hand and read it. "Where did you find this?"

"Stuck on the outside of the storage room in the garage. That's also where I found Dale. Someone shoved him from behind and locked him in."

Cassandra squeezed his hand. "Sweetie, you're tired, discouraged, and hungry. I'll bet you haven't had anything to eat today. Have you?"

Skip shook his head.

"Please come eat. You won't do Stephanie any good if you don't take care of yourself."

"You're right." Holding hands, they strolled toward the house. But before they reached the front door, a line of cars streamed onto the property. The sheriff and twelve other men hustled into the house after Skip and Cassandra.

"No sign of the little one yet?" asked Sheriff Robins.

Skip shook his head. "No trace of Stephanie anywhere."

"Do you have a picture of her?"

Skip pulled Stephanie's photo from his wallet.

"She's a pretty little thing." The sheriff passed around the photo.

"That's not all," said Skip. "Someone shoved Dale into the storage room in the garage and locked the door. They stuck this note on the door." He handed the sticky note to the sheriff.

As Skip expounded on the events of the past twenty-four hours, the sheriff listened intently.

Sheriff Robins raised an eyebrow. "Oh my. This sounds far more serious than I originally thought when you called me last night."

"We didn't realize how dangerous the situation might get until Stephanie disappeared, and we found that note. And we still don't know if Woody's disappearance is somehow related."

Sheriff Robins addressed his men. "Fellows, fan out, but stay in pairs! Cover this entire property, inside and out. Let's find that child. Look for any trap doors or secret passageways. Some of these old houses had them."

"Cassandra, I'm going to help them. Why don't you go eat lunch with Dale and your Aunt Mabel?"

Tears flooded her eyes and sudden sobs threatened to choke her. This was her fault. It was *all* her fault. Releasing Skip's arm, she spun around and dashed out the door.

Chapter 34

While Waiting for the Sheriff

Skip stared at her in bewilderment.

"What's with her?" asked Dale.

"I don't know." With a weary sigh, he hurried out the door after her. "Cassie?"

She bolted toward the barn. Skip trotted after her, pushing through the red, wooden door. The sounds of muffled sobs drifted down from above. Climbing the ladder to the loft, he crawled over to her and pulled her into a tender embrace.

Cassandra burst into tears. "Oh, Skip, I'm sorry. I'm sorry. I should have kept Stephanie with me. It's my fault." She buried her face in his shirt, sobbing uncontrollably.

"It wasn't your fault." Skip held her while she wept. "It wasn't your fault."

Tears coursed down his cheeks as he pondered the plight of his young sister. If he hadn't brought Stephanie to Woody's ranch, she would be safe at home right now.

"Skip, let's pray that God sends His angels to protect Stephanie and Uncle Woody."

Skip nodded. With his arms around Cassandra, he clutched her tightly and closed his eyes. "Lord Jesus, words cannot express our fear of what has become of Stephanie and Woody. Please send a host of angels to guard and protect them. Keep them safe and lead us to them, because only You know where they are. And should we not find them alive, I am thankful that they both know You as their Lord and Savior. We can trust Your promise that we'll be reunited again in heaven for all eternity."

"Skip, how could you even pray such a thing?"

Skip swallowed hard and fought back a new rush of tears. "Cassie, you and I both know that possibility exists. But don't you appreciate knowing that your Uncle Woody has accepted Jesus as his Savior?"

Cassandra nodded through her tears.

"And Stephanie asked Jesus into her heart when she was six. But don't lose hope. God is still in charge. First Corinthians chapter eight says that there is one God. He controls everything. According to verse six, He *is* everything."

"Skip, do you think they're still alive?"

"I hope so. To tell you the truth, I'm trying not to ponder on it."

Cassandra wiggled out of his arms and started down the ladder. "Let's go back to the house and find out if the sheriff has learned anything."

Returning to the house, Cassandra detoured into the dining room while Skip met Sheriff Robins coming down the staircase.

"Nothing," he said. "We practically tore this house apart looking for any evidence of a secret passageway."

Skip pushed his hands into his pockets and looked around the room. "But there's got to be one."

"I'm sure there is, but it's well hidden. Skip, my men searched every inch of this farmland. I've sent them out to expand the search for your sister."

Rejoining them, Cassandra handed Skip a plate of food, which he absently placed on the coffee table. "Well, I'm convinced that she's in this house somewhere, and I'm not leaving until I find her."

"Agreed. You and I will set up a twenty-four hour surveillance. Whoever is responsible will have to show themselves eventually."

"Can I stay?" called Dale from the dining room.

Sheriff Robins shook his head. "Afraid not, Dale. You could get hurt."

Cassandra gasped. "Get hurt! I don't want Skip to stay. What if he gets hurt?"

Grasping Cassandra's hand, Skip sat down on the sofa and pulled her into his lap. "Cassandra, what made you first notice me?"

"Your police uniform."

"What made you want to go out with me?"

Dale and Mabel drew near to hear her answer.

"My dad was in prison. I'd seen the effects of crime destroy my family, and I respected everything you stood for."

"Sometimes you smother me with protection. Would you prefer me to quit standing for what's right?"

"No."

"But police work is dangerous, and I could get hurt."

Cassandra sat quietly for a moment, and Skip knew she was pondering his statement. "I think I understand now. If I try to prevent you from doing something that could be dangerous, I'm smothering you with protection. But if you do it and get hurt, it's okay to show you lots of concern and affection."

Skip felt the heat rush to his face and knew that statement caused him to blush. "That's right, Cassandra."

The sheriff started for the door. "Well, Skip, I need to go secure my office and gather a few things for a night or two out here. I'll be back in a little bit."

"Okay."

Still sitting on his lap, Cassandra picked up his plate. "Open up. You'll need your strength."

Gazing into her tender brown eyes, Skip considered wrestling her for the plate, but then he might set it down again. After a moment of deliberation, he opted to take the path of least resistance, and he opened his mouth for her, allowing her the satisfaction of feeding him. Halfway through his meal, a frantic pounding rattled the front door.

Scrambling off his lap, Cassandra deposited his plate on the coffee table and raced Dale to the front door, swinging it open. One of Woody's ranch hands stood on the front step, practically white as a sheet.

Mabel rushed in from the kitchen. "Tony, what is it?"

"Two of the stallions got into a fight over a filly. When we tried to separate them, Arnie fell off his horse and broke his arm in a couple places. Mabel, it's a real bad break. He's going into shock. We can't reach the doctor. He needs medical attention right now, and we don't know what to do."

"Okay, get back to the ranch. I'll be right there." Mabel turned to her niece. "Cassandra, we have to go, and I'll probably need your assistance. How much first aid do you know?"

"None." Cassandra grinned sheepishly.

"None?"

"I know first aid," said Dale. "I've even delivered calves and other baby animals."

Mabel looked at Skip with concern. "I hate the thought of leaving you alone with all that's happened here, but it's not safe for Cassandra, and I'll need Dale."

"I'll be fine. The sheriff should be back soon."

"Skip, please be careful," said Cassandra. "We'll be praying for you and Stephanie and Uncle Woody."

Cupping her face in his hands, he kissed her and whispered in her ear, "I love you."

With teary eyes, Cassandra glanced at him one last time before hurrying out the door after Mabel and Dale. Skip watched from the window as she climbed into the back seat of the car, and they drove away.

"He's alone," said Kyle. "This may be our last chance to escape. If we're real quiet, we should be able to get by him. If we don't go now, we'll have to get by him *and* the sheriff, and I promise you, it won't be easy getting by the sheriff."

"It won't be easy getting by Skip."

"No, it won't, but it's our best chance, so we need to give it a shot. Just be quiet, and do exactly as I say."

Rusty rolled his eyes.

Skip glanced around. The house was deathly quiet. He eyed his unfinished plate sitting on the coffee table. Right now, he had no appetite, so he had no desire to finish his lunch. Pulling up his trouser leg, Skip unstrapped his gun from his ankle holster. He thought he'd do a little exploring while waiting for the sheriff to return. Moving silently from room to room, Skip held his gun ready. The upstairs was still.

Creeping back down the stairs, he tip-toed down the hallway, cautiously stepping into Doug's room. Hearing a muffled noise behind him, Skip spun around. There stood Linda's brother, Rusty.

Rusty knocked Skip's gun from his hand and swung at him. Skip ducked. Seizing Rusty's arm, he twisted it behind his back and forced him to the floor on his stomach.

"Where's my sister? Where's Stephanie? What did you do with her?"

A second man leaped on him from behind, knocking him to the floor. Skip kicked him back against the dresser and rolled, leaping up. As ceramic car models crashed to the floor, the two men scrambled to their feet and tackled him, landing on top of him and pinning his arms to the floor.

"Sheriff!"

"Shut up." Rusty belted him across the face, sending his glasses flying.

The two men jerked Skip to his feet. Swinging his leg behind Rusty, Skip shoved him backwards. Then he spun around and kneed his accomplice in the stomach. When the man released him, Skip kicked him into the dresser, shattering the lamp as it crashed to the floor.

Scrambling to his feet, Rusty leaped onto Skip's back and wrapped his right arm around his neck, applying enough pressure to cut off his oxygen.

Unable to breathe, Skip struggled to free Rusty's arm from around his neck. Then darkness descended all around him.

Chapter 35

The Great Escape

Kyle knelt beside the unconscious lad. He was breathing, and his pulse was strong. Rusty just cut off his oxygen long enough to make him pass out. With a sigh of frustration, he looked up at his partner. "Good job, Rusty. Even while we're escaping, you manage to take a hostage."

"Look. The kid's unconscious. The sheriff hasn't returned yet. Let's just leave him and get out of here while we have the chance."

"And what do you think the sheriff will do when he comes looking for this boy and finds him unconscious?"

"Look, Kyle. I'm sorry. Okay?"

"And why'd you hit him?" Kyle rose to his feet. "There are two of us, and we're both bigger than he is."

"I did it to shut him up," yelled Rusty. "He was calling for the sheriff."

"The sheriff isn't here. Everyone else has left the house. Nobody could hear him yell. And you belted him across the face to keep him quiet? If you had stayed put like I told you to, none of this would have happened."

"I said I'm sorry."

"It's too late, Rusty. Now we have another hostage, all because of your stupidity. We can't leave him here to tell what he knows. He can identify both of us."

After fighting with Skip, Kyle knew that they couldn't risk him getting loose. They had to tie him up good. Hoisting him into a fireman's carry, he carried the lad down the ladder and gently laid him on the floor. Rusty followed him down and closed the trap door behind them.

Kyle caught sight of the terror in Stephanie's blue eyes, and she started crying when she saw her brother brought down unconscious. Kyle blindfolded him while Rusty strapped his legs together. After smoothing a heavy piece of masking tape over his mouth, the men positioned him with his back up against a steel beam and bound his wrists together behind it.

"Now what?" said Rusty.

"We wait for the sheriff. When he sees that mess upstairs in Doug's room, he'll know this kid put up one tremendous fight, and he'll leave to bring back reinforcements. That's when we make our escape."

Rusty sighed. "Man, I hate to leave all this good stuff. We must have thousands of dollars in good, salable merchandise, even without the television that little kid kicked off the table."

"I know, but it's worthless if we can't get it out of here."

"What about them?" asked Rusty.

"Forget about them. They'll be found soon enough."

Kyle motioned for silence, listening to the small speaker Doug had set up in a corner of their underground hideout.

"Skip," called the sheriff. "Hey, Skip, where are you?"

They heard him gasp.

"Oh, my goodness."

"He's right above us in Doug's room," said Rusty.

"Oh, Skip, how can I break this news to Cassandra? I'll take care of that later. I need help. Maybe Jenson will loan me his dogs."

"Dogs," echoed Kyle and Rusty.

"Kyle, we got to get out of here, and we got to do it now."

"And a hostage will help us make it all the way to Australia. Untie that little girl. We're taking her with us."

Popping open his pocketknife, Rusty jerked Stephanie to her feet and sliced the rope that bound her wrists.

Stephanie tore the tape off her mouth and screamed. "Let me go! Let me go!" Kicking Rusty in the shin, she jerked away and dashed to Skip, throwing her arms around her brother and embracing him tightly.

"Get away from him, you little brat." Rusty seized her by the arm.

"Leave me alone!" Stephanie clung to Skip.

"Rusty, get that child quiet. The sheriff's still in the house."

"I'll get her quiet all right." Rusty pulled out his gun.

"Not that way, you idiot."

Ignoring Kyle, Rusty knelt down near Stephanie and Skip, holding up his gun for her to see.

"You know what this is?"

Stephanie nodded.

"Would you like to see what it can do?" Rusty held the barrel of the gun to Skip's head.

Skip tensed and turned his head.

"Shall I pull the trigger or will you be quiet?"

Stephanie swallowed hard. "I'll be quiet, but I'm not going with you." Her arms around Skip, she clutched his shirt and lay her head on his shoulder.

Kyle hurried over to them. "Okay, the sheriff's gone. My guess is that he'll be back in thirty minutes or less, so we don't have much time. Come here, Stephanie. I want to talk to you."

"No."

Rusty unbuckled his belt and jerked it out of the belt loops. "Why, you impudent, little brat."

"Go ahead and beat me. I'm still not going with you."

Rusty folded his belt in half. "Good, because I wasn't going to hit you." Skip winced when Rusty struck him with the belt.

"Stop it."

"Oh, Rusty, cut it out." Kyle snatched the belt away. "Come here, Stephanie. I'm not going to hurt you. I just want to talk to you." He held out his hand.

Stephanie glanced from Skip to Rusty to Kyle. Slowly rising to her feet, she followed him a few steps away.

"Stephanie, Rusty and I did a dumb thing and got ourselves into a real mess. We need you to help us get out of it. Now, you're going with us."

"I don't want to go." Stephanie started crying again.

"I know you don't, but I'll take real good care of you. And as soon as we land in Australia, I'll send you home."

"I can't leave Skip."

"You don't have a choice. Now, shall we shoot your brother and take you with us anyway, or will you go voluntarily?"

Stephanie exploded into an uncontrollable sob. "Don't hurt my brother. Please don't hurt him."

"I think that depends on you. Doesn't it?"

"Okay. I'll go with you. Just don't hurt Skip."

"Stephanie, consider yourself my niece from Ohio. So from now on, you refer to me as Uncle Kyle."

Stephanie wiped her eyes with the back of her hand and nodded.

Kyle winked at her. "Good girl. Now, we have to leave before the sheriff returns, or we'll never get out of here. Go hug and kiss your brother good-bye so we can go."

Tears trickling down her cheeks, Stephanie ran to Skip and embraced him. "Skip, I love you," she whispered in his ear. "I'm going to Australia with Uncle Kyle." She kissed him and dashed off.

Grabbing her small hand, Kyle hustled her to the ladder. He stopped suddenly and turned around, twisting the house key off Doug's key ring. "Here's the house key, Woody." He tossed it across the room. It clanked to the floor and slid under a new television. "We won't need it any more. Thanks for letting us borrow it."

Rusty, Kyle, and Stephanie scrambled up the ladder. Kyle slid aside a dead bolt and pushed open the trap door, which led into the closet of Doug's room.

"Out," he said. "Hurry up."

Stephanie crawled out the closet door, Rusty and Kyle behind her. She watched as Kyle dropped the trap door. Lifting up a small corner of the carpet that covered the door, he secured a heavy latch that locked the door shut. Stephanie started crying. Only a corner of that carpet wasn't nailed to the trap door and once it was laid back in place, it was next to impossible to see a difference. Skip hadn't found her, and the sheriff wouldn't find him.

"Oh, quit your sniveling," said Rusty. "I'm not traveling with a cry baby."

"And we're not traveling with an old grouch," said Kyle. "You pick on her again, and you're on your own. I've got enough trouble without you fighting with a child. Let's go, Stephanie."

Grasping her hand, Kyle led the way outside, crossed the yard to the detached garage, and lifted Stephanie into the cab of Doug's pickup truck. As the truck backed out, Rusty shut the garage doors and climbed in beside Stephanie. Kyle spun the truck around and headed for the main road.

"Are you okay?" he asked Stephanie.

Stephanie nodded. "I'm afraid that Skip will die down there before they find him."

"No way, missy. The sheriff will find him. I just hope he doesn't find Skip too soon. I'd like to be in the air by the time he does."

Chapter 36

The Hostage Dilemma

The last thing Skip remembered was Rusty pressing his arm securely against his wind pipe. He couldn't breathe. The next thing he knew, Stephanie was screaming, and she threw her arms around him.

Skip struggled against his bonds, but to no avail. Frustrated anger seethed through him, knowing he was helpless to protect his little sister or prevent them from taking her with them. But they couldn't take her to Australia. Stephanie didn't have a passport. So where were they *really* taking her?

Bending his knees, he kicked himself back against the support beam in hopes of relieving some of the strain on his aching arms.

Where was he? An attic? A basement? Considering everything he'd heard, Skip suspected he was still in the house somewhere. Likely in an underground room, because when the men left with Stephanie, it sounded like they *climbed* a wooden ladder.

Oh, Lord, am I in trouble. Please protect Stephanie. Keep her safe. Show the sheriff where we are because I doubt he'll find us without Your guidance. And keep Cassandra from worrying. She'll go crazy when she finds out.

Skip's mouth was dry, and he felt hot. Swallowing hard and trembling slightly, he scanned his memory for the scripture verse he learned when Cassandra's father had threatened his life.

Psalm 34:17 'The righteous cry out and the Lord hears, and delivers them out of all their troubles.' After repeating the verse several times, he said a prayer in his heart for his little sister, his young wife, Uncle Woody, and himself.

Lord, I need you. Psalm 46:1 says that You are my refuge and strength, a very present help in time of trouble. Well, I'm in trouble, and I need Your help. Skip pondered his situation. *Come to think of it, Lord, I'm always in trouble.*

Woody couldn't take his eyes off Skip. It grieved him to sit there listening to Rusty and Kyle gang up on him upstairs, but there was nothing he could do to stop it. Relieved to see Skip shift positions, Woody was thankful that the lad had regained consciousness.

Sitting against the wall on the other side of the room with the other hostage, a young woman not much older than Skip, he squirmed uncomfortably. His back hurt from sitting on concrete for two days. His arms ached from being tied behind him. His mouth was dry. With tape covering his mouth, he'd hardly had a sip of water since they'd grabbed him. And although their legs were strapped together, he and the girl weren't blindfolded or tied to anything, like Skip.

Woody exchanged glances with the girl. In the past two days, they'd had almost no opportunity to untie each other. Most of the time, they kept company with one or both of their abductors, affording them little chance of breaking free. Now that they were alone, without having to worry about the return of their captors, Woody and the girl turned back to back.

Woody struggled against his ropes, attempting to untie the girl. After several minutes, he realized it was useless, so he shifted positions and rolled to his stomach right behind her. Putting his face down by her hands, he rubbed his taped mouth against her fingers.

Fingering the edge of the tape, she worked to pry loose a corner of it. After several minutes, she managed to peel the tape up enough to grab onto it. With tears in his eyes, Woody pulled away from her, tearing the tape off his mouth.

"Ouch. I just yanked off two days of beard." He struggled to sit back up. "Skip, are you all right?"

Skip nodded.

"I was awfully worried about you. You were out cold when they brought you down." Woody turned to the girl. "Missy, if you'll lie down behind me, I will attempt to get that tape off your mouth."

Without any further prompting, she rolled to her stomach right behind him. Sliding his fingers around the edge of the tape, he gently pried up the corner and grasped it tightly. The girl pulled away from him, ripping the tape off her mouth.

With a big sigh, she maneuvered herself into a sitting position once again. "What a relief. Thank you. You think you can unstrap my legs?"

Woody glanced over at the strap. "It's Velcro. It'll be a breeze. Swing your legs around here." Feeling behind him, Woody peeled apart the Velcro. "So what's your name?"

"Michelle Hunter."

"I'm Woody McKenzie. You seem like a nice girl." He and Michelle shifted positions so she could unstrap his legs. "How did you get mixed up in all this?"

Michelle sighed. Feeling for the strap, she pried it apart, freeing Woody's legs. "You wouldn't believe me if I told you."

"Try me."

"Well, Doug Benson was a friend of mine. At least, that's what I thought."

Woody studied Skip from across the room. With his knees bent, the lad rested his head against the steel post.

"Turn around, Michelle. Let's try to loosen these ropes again."

Sitting back to back with Woody, Michelle attempted to loosen the ropes that secured his wrists together.

"I lived with my sister. Doug told me that he was into the stock market and could double my money for me. I believed him. I emptied my savings account and convinced my sister to do the same. Between the two of us, we gave Doug more than a hundred thousand dollars to invest. That was two days ago. The instant I realized that he was a crook, I called the sheriff, and he informed me that Doug was already in custody. I told the sheriff about the money, but he said I'd probably never see it again."

"Does your sister know?"

"Yes. She was so mad, she kicked me out. I only hope that Doug got arrested before he got to the bank. I immediately called off work and came here to look for that money."

"Michelle, do you suppose that's the money Rusty and Kyle were searching for?"

"I have no doubt. Thank goodness they didn't find it. Anyway, when I got here, and I saw all these poor farm animals that no one was caring for, I started to feed them. That is, until I realized I wasn't alone. Those two bullies dragged me down here and tied me up." Unable to loosen the ropes, Michelle gave up. "I can't do it, Woody. I'm sorry."

"Well, we mustn't give up. I'll try to untie you again."

While Woody fumbled with Michelle's securely knotted rope, the sheriff arrived with what sounded like an army. Woody and Michelle listened intently to the activity above them as it was piped down through the small speaker.

"Skip? Woody? Anybody?" called the sheriff. "If you can hear me, answer!"

"They won't hear us unless they're in Doug's closet," said Woody. "This place is too sound tight."

Chapter 37

Fishing for Information

Splitting up, the search party dismantled the rooms, piece by piece, in search of a hidden passageway or secret room.

"Hey, Sheriff, Craig's here with his dogs."

"Great. Let him in."

"Hi, Kasey." Craig Jenson extended his hand. "Haven't seen you in ages."

Sheriff Robins grasped his hand firmly. "Thanks for coming, Craig. I'm sorry we couldn't have gotten together under more pleasant circumstances."

"Don't worry about it. That's what friends are for."

Kasey briefed Craig on the situation and passed him two small zipper bags. "I stopped by Woody's ranch on my way back out here and picked up two clothing items: one from Stephanie and one from Woody."

Craig took the plastic bags. "You handled these carefully, I presume."

"Oh, yeah. I made sure not to contaminate them with my smell or anyone else's."

"Good." Not wanting to confuse his dogs, Craig allowed them to sniff only Stephanie's clothing item. The dogs ran through the house, sniffing. When they came to Doug's room, they scratched at the closet door.

"Someone in there, boy?" Kasey opened the door.

The dogs entered the closet, sniffing and pawing the carpet on the floor. Silently kneeling down, the sheriff felt the floor for loose boards. He pounded on the closet wall and rummaged through the things on the shelf. With a heavy sigh, he stepped out of the closet.

"Come on, fellows. There's nothing in there." Calling the dogs out, he shut the door.

To his surprise, the dogs followed a scent along the floor leading to the front door. He opened the door, and the dogs led them across the yard and into the garage. Kasey and Craig trailed them. Once inside, they wandered in circles, and Kasey knew they lost the scent.

"I don't like this," said Kasey. "Did someone take that child away in a car?"

"Sure looks that way," said Craig. "Let's give the dogs a new scent and see if they can track Woody."

To their dismay, the dogs had trouble picking up his scent and finally wandered to the same closet.

"What do you make of that?" asked Kasey.

Craig shrugged. "I haven't any idea."

Needing a little fresh air, Kasey called everyone outside. "Has anyone turned up anything?"

Everyone shook their heads.

"Well, they're here somewhere." The sheriff slammed his right fist into his left palm. "We'll stake out the house and wait. They have to come out of hiding eventually. I need as many as can stay. Who is willing and able?"

Every hand shot up, including Craig's.

"Good." The sheriff counted his volunteers. "I want teams of two stationed all over this house. We'll wait them out."

Kyle parked the truck at the Fenton Regional Airport.

"Well, this is our stop, sweetheart." He grasped her hand and led her into the terminal, where he purchased three air fares for Los Angeles, with a stop in Cheyenne."

The threesome sat down at Gate 2 to wait for their flight to board.

Rusty looked at Kyle. "You had to buy tickets? I thought you booked our flights already."

"I did. But I was an idiot and booked them from Los Angeles to Australia. So we still need to get to L.A."

Rusty laughed. "Well, at least I'm not the only one who makes idiotic mistakes. Speaking of which, doesn't Stephanie need a passport to go to Australia?"

"Why would she need a passport? She's under 12."

Sitting between Kyle and Rusty, Stephanie puckered. "Why do I have to go with you? Why can't you just get on the plane without me? I want Skip." Stephanie burst into tears.

"Here we go again," said Rusty. "All she does is talk about her brother and cry."

"Shh, don't cry," said Kyle. "Your brother is all right, and so are you. We need you to help us get out of the country. Remember? As soon as we land in Australia, we'll send you back on the first available flight."

"How long will it take us to get to Australia?"

"A real long time, because this plane won't take us there."

"Why not?"

"Because this is only a regional airport. To get to Australia, we have to fly out of an international airport. We'll get on a small plane here, change planes in Cheyenne, and fly to an international airport where we'll change planes again."

Skip listened to the conversation coming from across the room. Too bad they forgot about him. Woody had said that no one would hear them yell from that underground room unless they were practically in Doug's closet. Well, the sheriff just searched the closet for a hidden panel or trap door. It was an ideal time for Woody and Michelle to yell for help or make some noise, but they were so involved in their discussion that they didn't notice. And with his mouth taped shut, he couldn't even alert them to the sheriff's nearness.

"I'm not getting anywhere with these ropes," said Woody. "Let me help Skip."

It's about time, although it's a little late.

Skip winced when he felt the blindfold tugged off his head, squeezing his eyes shut against the sudden brightness. Woody's calloused fingers brushed his tender cheek when he peeled up a corner of the tape and tore it off his mouth.

"Thanks, Woody." Squinting from the light, Skip blinked and looked up at him. "It's mighty good to see you."

"Boy, do you have a shiner. Rusty really belted you hard. You didn't come home looking half this bad after brawling with Doug."

"Maybe not, but I sure felt it. All my bruises from that fight are underneath my shirt."

"Oh." Woody maneuvered himself to remove the Velcro strap around Skip's legs.

"You and Michelle weren't tied to anything?" asked Skip.

"Nope. We were only in the way. They considered you a threat."

With his legs now unrestricted, Skip pushed himself back against the post to relieve some of the strain on his arms. He looked at Michelle, pondering her story and wondering if she had overheard him and Dale talking about the money they'd found. But then, wouldn't Rusty, Kyle, and Woody also know about it? Considering that thought, Skip went fishing for information.

"We can hear everything that's going on upstairs. They must have planted bugs in every room."

"Actually, from listening to them talk, we learned that Doug wired the house like this in order to keep a tight rein on his brother," said Woody. "Doug always knew where Dale was, what he was doing, and who he was talking to. He scattered these devices throughout the house, but there are none in the library because Dale was forbidden to go into it. Doug usually kept it locked up."

"Yeah, that's what Dale was telling me."

"Last night, we heard you and Dale come into the house. Kyle was fixing to search the library for that money when you boys arrived. It was the second time you surprised him, and he didn't have time to lock it up. Rusty was furious. They didn't like it when you kids went into that room because they couldn't hear anything."

"It's quiet upstairs." Skip looked upward, listening intently.

"The search party must have left."

"Sure seems that way," said Skip. "But they'll be back, and we need to be ready when they get back."

Woody looked baffled. "Uh ... Okay. So how do we get ready?"

"This beam I'm tied to is metal, and it connects to the ceiling. My car keys are in my pocket. If we banged them against it, the noise would attract attention."

"Hm. Can you stand up?"

"I think so." Forcing himself back against the beam, Skip pushed himself into a standing position.

Woody studied Skip's trousers. "Which pocket are they in?"

"My right."

"I'll see if I can grab them."

Struggling to her feet, Michelle approached them.

"Stand still, Skip," said Woody.

"I'm trying, but you're tickling me."

"Got 'em! Oops, I just dropped them."

"Woody, would you hurry up and get out of my pocket."

"Just a minute. This isn't easy with my hands tied. This pocket is deep. What else do you have in it?"

"Just my mouse trap."

"Mouse trap."

Woody yanked his hand out of Skip's pocket, and Skip exploded into laughter. Looking up, he spotted the girl watching him.

"Hi, I'm Skip. Please forgive me for not offering you my hand."

"Sorry for not introducing you," said Woody. "I've been a little preoccupied."

"Doing what?" asked Skip.

"Ooo, if my hands weren't tied behind my back, I'd turn you over my knee and spank you."

"I wish you could. Then at least one of us would be untied."

"Excuse me, gentlemen. I'm ready to get out of here. Woody, would you get those keys so we can make some noise that will be heard?"

"She's right," said Woody. "Skip, hold still this time."

"Yes, sir."

Slipping his hand into Skip's pocket, Woody once again attempted to grab his keys. Skip winced and squirmed. It tickled. With Woody focused on retrieving those keys, he obviously overlooked Skip's squirming.

"Got 'em." With a sigh of relief, he carefully withdrew the keys from Skip's pocket. "Well, I'm ready to rattle these keys against this post, but we might as well hold off. No one's up there to hear it. We'll wait until the search party returns."

"I hope it's soon," said Michelle.

Skip sighed. "I do, too. My arms ache something fierce. But I fear that they've already given up looking for us."

"No. Kasey hates unfinished business. He'll be delighted to discover all this stolen merchandise. Here, Skip, hold the keys. I'll see if I can loosen the ropes some."

With his back to the post, Woody felt the ropes and fingered the knots, trying to loosen them enough for Skip to slip his hands out.

Chapter 38

The Key to Rescue

Sitting by the window with Kyle and Rusty occupying the other two seats, Stephanie gazed toward the sky. It was time she prayed. Skip had once told her that God would hear her prayer no matter where she was, and she didn't even have to pray out loud, because He could also hear her thoughts.

Lord, help me know what to do. I don't want to go to Australia. I need to get away from these two bad men. Show me how. And take care of Skip. Help the sheriff find him.

The plane arrived in Cheyenne shortly before sunset, and Stephanie sullenly dragged herself down the aisle, following them through the breezeway. With only minutes to catch their connecting flight to Los Angeles, Rusty and Kyle grabbed her hands and ran through the terminal.

Just then, a thought popped into her head. "Uncle Kyle, I have to go to the bathroom."

"Again? You just went."

"That was at the last airport."

Kyle sighed. "Okay, but hurry up." He released Stephanie's hand and watched her dash into the women's restroom.

Stephanie raced through the bathroom in search of another exit, but there was none. She had hoped to escape through a different door than the one she'd entered. She saw it in a movie once. With a sorrowful sigh, she spun around and returned to Kyle and Rusty.

"Boy, that was fast."

"I decided to wait until we got to Los Angeles."

"Okay. We'd better hurry, or we'll miss our connecting flight." With the child between them, Kyle and Rusty grasped her hands and raced to the departure gate.

"We just made it." Rusty settled back in his seat. "One more plane, and we're home free."

Kasey's six teams silently settled into surveillance positions throughout the house. Nobody talked. Everybody listened, waited, and watched. The sun dropped below the horizon, and the house grew dark.

Tired of sitting quiet for so long in the dark, one of the men flipped on a nearby lamp. His partner gasped.

"Hey, Joe, do you see that? Look."

Crawling to the nearby table, the man reached under it and snapped off a small metal box.

"A listening device."

"Skip, do you hear that?" Woody snatched the keys from him and wildly rapped them on the metal beam.

"They've probably been up there the entire time."

"What's that noise?" asked Joe.

"What noise?"

"Listen. Don't you hear it?"

"No, but whatever it is, it's not as important as showing this to the sheriff."

"Oh, no," said Skip. "They're not paying any attention."

"They will. We mustn't give up, because it may be our only hope."

Listening intently to what was transpiring upstairs, they heard the two members of the search team telling the sheriff about the transmitter they'd found.

"No wonder we could never catch them," said Sheriff Robins. "I'll bet these things are scattered all over this house. Call the other guys. Let's search this place for more bugs."

"We've searched this house half a dozen times, Kasey. How come we didn't discover this device sooner?" asked Joe.

"Because we weren't looking for something so small. We were looking for missing people and great big hideaways."

Gathering together his surveillance teams, the sheriff sent them throughout the house searching for tiny transmitters. One by one, the transmitters were disabled. It distressed Skip that the sheriff's men were so preoccupied with their search that they seemed to overlook the soft clanking noise.

"It's no use," said Michelle. "They don't hear it."

"How do we know that?" asked Skip. "We don't know what's going on upstairs any more."

With a frustrated sigh, Woody smacked the keys against the metal with renewed vengeance.

Kasey looked all around him, listening intently to the soft clanging sound and trying to localize it. "Craig, what's that noise?"

"What noise?"

"Listen."

Craig listened carefully.

"Do you hear it?" asked Kasey.

"Yeah, what do you suppose it is?"

"I don't know, but I think we need to find out."

Once again, Kasey gathered together his men and learned that several others had also heard the noise. "All right, fellows, let's spread out and find out where that noise is coming from. We've looked in all the obvious places. Start looking in the unobvious. Look for trap doors and false panels. Put your ears against the walls, inside the closets, on the floor. And nobody goes alone. Now, move out!"

The search party scattered throughout the house in teams of twos and threes. Dropping down on the sofa, Kasey rested his elbows on his knees and buried his face in his hands.

"Tired, Kasey?" Craig rested his hand on his friend's shoulder and sat down beside him.

"Discouraged." Looking up, he gazed across the room at the dogs napping in the corner. Kasey leaped to his feet. "Craig, how could we have missed it? The dogs led us right to them."

He bolted down the hall, Craig on his heels, and they darted into Doug's room. Kasey jerked open the closet door, dropped to the floor, and placed his ear against the carpet. He sat up and looked at Craig.

"Either that noise is coming from under the house or this place has a basement." Pulling out his pocketknife, he poked and prodded the carpet. "Well, looky there." Prying up the piece of carpet, Kasey popped the latch on the trap door and slowly opened it up. "No wonder we couldn't find it."

"Be careful, Kase."

"I doubt there's anything to worry about now. This trap door was locked from the outside. That means our notorious bandits have already made their getaway."

Slowly descending the ladder, he dropped to the floor. Craig followed him. With a grin, Kasey trotted over to the three captives.

"Sheriff, are we ever glad to see you," said Skip.

"I'll say, we are," said Woody.

Withdrawing his pocketknife, Kasey sliced the ropes, freeing Skip, Woody, and Michelle. "Where's the little one?"

"Gone. They left and took her with them." Woody handed Skip his keys.

"Did they say where they were headed?"

"Australia," said Skip. "They threatened to kill me unless she went with them willingly."

"When did they leave?"

"Shortly after you left to round up a search party to look for me," said Skip.

Kasey's eyes widened. "That was hours ago! Come on, fellows. Time is running out. Let's hurry." Leading the way up the ladder, he rounded up his men. "Our search is over, fellows. You guys did an outstanding job, and I appreciate your help."

Many hands slapped Woody's back in welcome. Skip shook hands with those who had given hours searching for him and Stephanie.

"Now, if you'll excuse us," said Kasey. "Our job isn't finished. The nine-year-old child was taken hostage, and we have work to do."

Following the Trail

The last to leave the farmhouse, Woody locked the front door before handing the house key to Sheriff Robins.

"Thanks. I'll need this. Now let's head into town. I have some phone calls to make, and you three have lots to fill me in on."

"That we do." Escorting Michelle to the sheriff's police car, Woody opened the back door for her. "Young lady, you can spend the night at our ranch house. Mabel won't mind, and we have more than enough room."

"Thank you. That's kind of you."

"Don't mention it." Woody and the sheriff opened the front doors simultaneously, preparing to climb into the cruiser.

Skip jerked to a stop beside the car. "Wait. My gun and glasses."

"Oh, I'm sorry," said the sheriff. He handed Skip his gun and pulled the glasses from his shirt pocket.

"Thank you, sir." Skip slid into the back seat of the sheriff's car, next to Michelle.

As they drove, Woody talked to the sheriff. "You were right, Kasey. Doug Benson was behind this whole racket. But after he got arrested, his two partners decided that they'd grab the rest of the stolen merchandise and cash in on it while they had a chance."

"Who did you say were his two partners?"

"A guy named Rusty ... I didn't know him ... and Kyle Carver."

"You're kidding! I've known Kyle for years. I would never have suspected him. He just doesn't seem the type. How do you suppose he got mixed up in something like this?"

"Beats me. I wouldn't have believed it if I hadn't seen it."

When the airplane finally touched down in Los Angeles, Stephanie choked back a lump in her throat and silently followed Kyle and Rusty off the plane. With each leg of their journey, she was getting further and further from home.

Tears pooled in her eyes. "Please don't take me to Australia. I don't want to go."

Sitting down on a bench, Kyle grasped her hand and drew her close to him. "Don't be afraid, Stephanie. We'll send you home as soon as we arrive. That's a promise."

"When do we get on the next plane?" Stephanie dried her eyes with the back of her hand.

"Not for awhile. We have a one-hour layover here."

"Does that mean that I have time to go to the bathroom?"

"Come on, I'll take you."

"It's only over there. I can go by myself."

Hurrying to the restroom, Stephanie shoved open the door and glanced around. The facilities were massive. Strolling around the corner, she spotted another exit, where she quietly slipped out. With a satisfied sigh, she disappeared into a crowd of people headed the opposite direction from where she'd left Rusty and Kyle waiting for her.

Reaching the sheriff's office, Skip blinked back tears, thankful that his dark glasses hid his watery eyes. If anything happened to his little sister, he would never forgive himself. Woody opened the back door for him and Michelle. Skip dragged himself from the car and trailed the others into the small-town police station. Michelle collapsed onto the vinyl sofa across from the sheriff's desk.

Sheriff Robins dropped into a comfortable armchair behind his desk and pulled out a pad and pen. "Okay,

Woody, what did the other man look like and how were the two of them dressed?"

Leaning on the desk, Woody related all he could remember about Kyle and Rusty. The sheriff scribbled notes before snatching up the phone and calling airport security. He put it on speakerphone so Skip and Woody could hear the conversation.

Sheriff Robins identified himself to the head of the security office and briefed him on the reason for his call. "They have a nine-year-old girl with them. Blue eyes and long, blonde hair. The child was abducted, and both men are wanted on felony charges. They're headed for Australia."

"Okay, Sheriff Robins. I'll check into it and call you back as soon as I learn anything."

"We'll be waiting for your call, Mr. Barkley." The sheriff disconnected the call.

"Sheriff, may I call Cassandra and tell her I'm all right?" asked Skip.

"If you'd like, but it's not necessary. She doesn't even know that you were missing."

"You didn't tell her?"

"Heavens, no. That girl would have gone hysterical. I had no intentions of telling her until I absolutely had to."

Woody snatched up the receiver. "Well, I will call Mabel." He punched in his phone number and waited. "Good to hear your voice, Mabel ... I'm calling from the sheriff's office ... It's a long story, dear. I'll tell you all about it when I get home ... Skip's okay. He's here with me, but Stephanie is still in the hands of her kidnappers. Pray for her, and we'll be home as soon as possible. I love you, dear. Bye."

No sooner had Woody hung up when the phone rang again. The sheriff grabbed it. "Sheriff Robins."

"This is Adam Barkley from the Fenton Regional Airport security. Kyle Carver and Rusty O'Sheif boarded Flight 153 for Cheyenne. They did have a little girl with them. We are already in touch with the Cheyenne airport."

After jotting down the information, Sheriff Robins dialed the Cheyenne airport, once again putting on the speakerphone. His call was patched through to the head of security.

"Sheriff Robins, this is Mark Riley at Cheyenne Airport Security. I've been expecting your call. I've located your two suspects. Rusty O'Sheif and Kyle Carver flew out on Sunrise Airways, flight 2061, headed for Los Angeles International Airport. I talked to a ticket agent near the gate who remembers seeing a little girl with them."

"When did their flight leave?"

"Two hours ago."

"Thanks, Mr. Riley." Calling LAX, the sheriff's concerned expression met Skip's teary gaze. "Skip, I fear we may be too late. Unless their flight had a layover in L.A., they're on their way to Australia right now."

"Not Stephanie. She doesn't have a passport. So what did they do with her?" Skip dropped into a nearby chair and buried his face in his hands.

"You all right, Skip?" asked Woody. "You're awfully pale."

"My little sister, Uncle Woody. They had my little sister. Where is she now?"

"She's in God's hands, son. And there is no one better qualified to care for her than He. Trust Him."

Chapter 40

The Search for Stephanie

When Stephanie didn't return within a reasonable amount of time, Kyle strolled over to the restroom, stopping the first lady that walked out.

"Excuse me, ma'am. Did you happen to see a little girl in there about nine or ten-years-old with blue eyes and blonde hair? She went in some time ago and hasn't come out yet."

"No, I'm sorry." The woman started to walk away, but Kyle stopped her.

"Please. She's my niece. Would you be so kind as to go check for me?"

"Oh, all right." The young woman disappeared back into the restroom and returned a moment later. "There are no little girls in there with blonde hair."

"Are you sure? I've been watching this door for twenty minutes."

"I'm sure. She probably went out the other door by mistake."

"Other door? What other door?"

"There's another exit on the other side of the restroom."

"There is? Oh, no." Kyle raced back to Rusty. "Rusty, Stephanie's taken off. We've got to find her."

Rusty glanced at his watch. "Kyle, our plane leaves in thirty minutes. Forget about her. We don't need her any more."

"And what if she goes to the airport police and tells them that we kidnapped her? What then?"

"So we deny it. Destroy her ticket. That way ... Wait a minute. When did you even purchase her an airline ticket to Australia?"

"Well, I didn't buy one specifically for Stephanie. But I paid for Doug's. I figure, she could use that one. That way, it doesn't go to waste."

Rusty laughed and shook his head. "You talk about *me* being an idiot. It doesn't work that way. She has to have one in her own name, like she did when she flew to L.A. And I'm almost positive, she needs a passport to go to Australia. Which means, we can't take her with us. We leave her here."

"We can't leave her here. I promised to send her home. Now get off your fat duff and help me find her."

"Find her yourself, Kyle. As far as I'm concerned, we should have dumped her in Cheyenne. She's nothing but extra baggage."

"*You're* the extra baggage. All you are is dead weight, Rusty. How did I ever get myself into this mess?" Spinning around, Kyle raced off in search of Stephanie.

Stephanie hurried through the crowded airport, frequently glancing behind her for any sign of Rusty or Kyle. Not watching where she was going, she walked right into an airport policeman. Scrambling back, Stephanie looked up at him.

"Oh, I'm sorry."

"Sweetheart, are you lost?"

"Lost? Well, um ..." Looking over her shoulder, she spotted Kyle. "No, sir. I was just on my way to the bathroom. Sorry." Ducking under the policeman's arm, she dashed into the restroom.

"Boy, that was a close one. If I said 'yes' that police officer would find Kyle and put me on that plane to Australia. If I can hide until their plane leaves, I'll be safe."

Sheriff Robins relayed the description of Stephanie's abductors to the airport police while Woody and Skip leaned anxiously on his desk. Hanging up the telephone, Kasey looked up at Skip. "There's nothing to do now but wait. You guys look exhausted. It's after midnight. Why don't you go home and get some sleep. I promise to call you as soon as I know anything."

"Sleep? Who can sleep?" said Skip. "I'd rather stay here because I would just lie awake anyway."

Woody yawned. "Well, I've hardly gotten any sleep the last two nights, and neither has Michelle."

"Here, Woody, take my car." Kasey fished his car keys from his trouser pocket and passed them to Woody. "You two go home, and get some rest."

"What about Skip?"

The sheriff stifled a yawn. "I'll bring him home in the squad car."

Woody slid his arm around Skip's shoulders. "Son, you haven't had much rest, either. Come home, and get some sleep. There's nothing more you can do for Stephanie tonight, anyway."

"Thank you, sir, but I think I'll stay here."

"Okay, Skip. Goodnight." With Kasey's keys in hand, Woody roused Michelle from a sound sleep and guided her out the door.

Kasey leaned back in his chair and propped his feet up on his desk. With a yawn, Skip removed his glasses to rub his eyes. Setting his glasses on the sheriff's desk, he collapsed onto the sofa, and his eyes dropped shut. Kasey studied the lad. Skip's steady breathing and relaxed posture indicated that he'd already drifted to sleep. Closing his eyes, Kasey dozed.

"Now boarding at gate 92, Sunrise Airlines, flight 2093, for Australia."

Rusty listened to the announcement over the public address system. Not waiting for Kyle, he grabbed his jacket and boarded the plane. Rusty took his seat next to the window and grinned. Anxious for the plane to take off, he watched as people filed down the aisle looking for their seats and rearranged the overhead compartments to make room for their bags. As passengers found their seats and the aisle cleared, he knew they were getting ready to taxi out. In a few minutes, he would be airborne and nearly home free.

Just then, an announcement came over the airplane's PA system.

"Ladies and gentlemen, I regret to inform you that we have been delayed for take off. Please be patient, and we will be leaving as soon as possible. Thank you."

"Delayed," cried Rusty. "Wonderful."

Gasping for breath, Kyle dropped into his seat beside his partner. "I couldn't find her. I looked everywhere. I ran all the way to get back before the plane left. Boy, I thought I'd missed it."

"You would have, but we've been delayed for take-off."

"Why?"

Rusty shrugged. "I don't know." He'd ask a stewardess. Glancing around for one, he gasped at the sight of four men running down the center aisle of the 757. Two of them were uniformed police officers, and they were all four armed.

Kyle looked at him just as the men reached them.

"Gentlemen, you're both under arrest. Please, come with us." The uniformed officers pulled them both to their feet, handcuffed them, and escorted them off the plane.

Once they had cleared the breezeway and re-entered the terminal, they were questioned. "Where's the little girl?" demanded one of the men in plain clothes.

"Stephanie Shaughnessy," added a uniformed officer. We know you had her. *Now where is she?*"

"We have no idea what you're talking about," said Rusty. "We're traveling alone! Now, you're going to make us miss our flight."

Kyle looked down at the floor, listening to them interrogate Rusty. Sticking to his story, Rusty sounded convincing. But it was obvious they weren't buying it.

"Get him out of here. Book him for kidnapping." The man glared at Rusty. "And if we don't find that child, we'll charge you with murder."

A uniformed officer led Rusty away, even while he maintained his innocence and protested his arrest.

Kyle looked up at the three remaining officers, not certain why they didn't drag him off with Rusty.

"All right, Kyle. Rusty's going down for kidnapping. You work with us, and we'll reduce the charges against you. You've got nothing to lose. Now where's Stephanie?"

Kyle sighed and looked at him. "I honestly don't know. She managed to get away from me."

"How?"

"She went into the restroom through one entrance and escaped through another. I didn't discover she'd run off for almost twenty minutes, because I was waiting for her at the door that she'd entered."

Stephanie peeked around the corner of the bathroom door. It looked safe. They had announced the boarding of her flight almost twenty minutes ago. Quietly slipping out the door, she looked both ways. There were people everywhere, heading in every direction, but no friendly faces. Not one.

"Stephanie?"

Stephanie glanced around to see who called her name.

An airport police officer approached her. "Are you Stephanie?"

Her eyes glazed over with fear. There was no doubt in her mind that Kyle had gotten the airport police to help him find her. But she was *not* going to Australia. Stephanie bolted, but the officer grabbed her arm.

"Hold on."

"Let me go." She kicked him in the shin and jerked free. Almost immediately, someone else grabbed her by the back of the britches, yanking her off her feet. *"Let me go. Help! Police!"* Dangling upside down, she swung her fists and kicked.

The uniformed man holding her by the waistband of her britches chuckled. "Missy, I don't know if I want to put you down after what you did to my partner."

Stephanie glanced over at him. Seeing a stripe down the leg of his trousers and a gun belt strapped to his waist, she stopped kicking.

"Little lady, if I set you down, will you behave yourself?"

"*No.* Because I'm not going to Australia with anybody, and *you can't make me.*"

"Australia? Stephanie, we're sending you home. Your brother is going crazy trying to locate you." The officer set her down. "You want to go home. Don't you?"

Sudden sobs of relief constricted Stephanie's throat, and she nodded her assent.

"Good. Let's go make arrangements for your return trip. Then we'll call Skip to let him know what time he can pick you up at the airport."

"Okay."

The police officer held out his hand, and she grasped it.

The rude jangle of the phone brought Kasey's boots crashing to the floor. He snatched up the receiver before it rang again.

"Sheriff Robins."

Skip leaped to his feet and leaned on the sheriff's desk.

"This is Mike Thompson at LAX. We've apprehended Kyle Carver and Rusty O'Sheif, and we have Stephanie Shaughnessy in our custody."

"Great!" The sheriff nodded to Skip who closed his eyes in a silent prayer of thanks.

"We've made arrangements for her return flight," said Mike. "She'll arrive at Fenton Regional Airport at 6:23 am, flight 242."

"We'll be there. Thanks, Mike." Replacing the receiver, the sheriff rose to his feet. "They've found your little sister, Skip. We have to leave here around six o'clock to pick her up from the airport. That gives us approximately four more hours to sleep. So I'm going to bed."

With a yawn, Skip dropped back onto the sofa. "Is it okay if I crash here?"

"Absolutely." Kasey tossed his guest a blanket and an extra pillow. Flipping off the overhead light, he shuffled into the other room, sat down on a twin-sized bed, and removed his boots. After setting the alarm clock, he lay down on top of the covers and pulled an extra blanket over himself, quickly dropping into a sound sleep.

Chapter 41

Returning Home

An airport security officer escorted Stephanie onto the plane and seated her in First Class. When the officer left, she unbuckled her seat belt and scooted into the window seat.

A moment later, a middle-aged woman sat next to her. "Airplanes are fascinating. Aren't they, dear?"

Stephanie glanced at her before looking out the window once again.

"Where are your parents? You're not traveling alone, are you? Especially not at this hour of the night."

Stephanie was tired. It had been a very long day, and she didn't feel like engaging in conversation, but she didn't want to be rude. With a sigh, she continued gazing out the window. "Yes, ma'am."

"Where are you going? To visit a relative?"

"No, ma'am. I'm going home."

"Oh, so you were visiting someone here in Los Angeles."

Stephanie looked at her. "I didn't visit nobody. I was kidnapped. And the kidnappers were going to take me to Australia. But the police caught them, and now they're sending me home."

"Oh, really? How did you get kidnapped?"

"I just went in to get a drink of water," said Stephanie. "And, then, I walked out of the kitchen and saw a man in the living room, so I screamed."

"I take it, he wasn't supposed to be there."

"No, ma'am. He grabbed me and put his hand over my mouth so I didn't scream again. Then he carried me down to the basement and tied me up. And when my brother came looking for me, he tied him up, too."

"Really."

"Yes. Then they decided to leave before the sheriff found them. They told me I had to come with them, or they would kill my brother."

"You don't say."

"You don't believe me. Do you?"

"Sweetheart, you have a wonderful imagination. But that's good for a youngster your age."

"It's not my imagination," said Stephanie. "It really happened."

"If you say so. What's your name?"

"Stephanie."

"You're kidding! That's my name, too. Actually, it's Stephanie Rose. My little brother always called me Stephanie, but I usually go by Rose."

"Stephanie Rose?" Stephanie enunciated each syllable. "My middle name is Rose, too."

"Is it, now?"

"Yes, ma'am, it is. Where are you going?"

"Forest Valley, to see my brother."

"That's where I live," said Stephanie.

Rose smiled at her, but didn't say anything.

"The police said my brother will meet me at the airport. I can hardly wait to see him. Will your brother meet you at the airport?" asked Stephanie.

Rose's smile faded, and she shook her head. "No, dear. He doesn't have any idea that I'm coming to see him."

"Why didn't you call or write and let him know?"

Rose sighed. "I haven't spoken to my brother in over twenty years. I thought if I warned him that I was coming, that he would reject me."

"Is he mad at you?"

"No, I was mad at him. You see, we were born and reared in Forest Valley, and he was my best friend. We did everything together. Only problem was, I hated that town. It was too small for me. I wanted to gain riches and honor and prestige with my new business idea, and I wanted my brother to be part of it, but not in Forest Valley. However, my brother loved that town. Nothing could get him to leave."

"So you got mad at him about that?" asked Stephanie.

Rose nodded. "Yeah. Pretty stupid, isn't it?"

"Kind of. So what happened with your idea?"

"My business flourished, and I have more money than I know what to do with. I married a wonderful man, but recently he passed away, and my two boys took off, so now I'm all alone again. Would you like to see some pictures of my family?" Rose withdrew a stack of photos from her purse. "These are my sons."

"That one's cute," said Stephanie.

"That's Robby, my youngest. He's seventeen. And this is my husband. And this is my brother, Stephen, when he was nineteen. It's the only picture I have of him."

Stephanie's eyes widened. "This is a picture of your brother?" She reached for the picture, studying it. "He looks just like my brother."

Rose smiled at her. "You're cute, Stephanie. You have the biggest imagination of any child I've ever met."

"But he does. When we land, you come with me to meet him. I will be so glad to see him. When I left, he was still tied up down in the basement."

Rose burst into giggles and shook her head.

"You don't believe a word I said. Do you?" demanded Stephanie.

"Oh, I believe that you believe it. But Stephanie, if you're honest, you'll admit that your story sounds a little far fetched."

"Yeah, I guess it does." Stephanie rubbed her eyes. With a yawn, she rested her head against the window and drifted off to sleep. When she awoke, the plane was on the ground. "Are we there already?"

"We're in Salt Lake City. Now, we have to change planes," said Rose.

A stewardess escorted Stephanie to her connecting flight. Once again, Rose joined her.

"Are you getting on this plane, too?" asked Stephanie.

"Of course. I'm on my way to Forest Valley, and Fenton is the nearest airport."

"May I please sit with you?"

"Certainly. Come on." Grasping Stephanie's hand, Rose led her onto the plane and to their seats.

Skip rubbed his eyes and yawned before sliding into the cruiser beside Sheriff Robins. "Sheriff, do you know that young woman that was held captive with me and Woody?"

"Yeah. She came into the office about three days ago. She said that Doug Benson swindled her out of a hundred thousand dollars, and she wanted me to get it back for her. I told her she'd probably never see it again, so she'll be thrilled that you recovered it."

Stephanie's one-hour flight seemed to take forever. As the plane taxied in, the nine-year-old gazed excitedly out the window. She was almost home.

"What's the matter, dear?" asked Rose.

Stephanie sighed. "I'm glad to be almost home. I can hardly wait to see my brother."

Rose embraced her. "I know the feeling."

"Rose, please come with me. I want you to meet him."

"Thank you, dear, but I'm in a hurry."

"Why? Your brother doesn't even know you're coming."

"That's true, but I know, and I can't wait to see him and reconcile. To beg his forgiveness for my stubbornness. He wrote me dozens of letters that I never answered. I know that he got married and had a son. He wrote to me for ten years after I stormed out on him."

Stephanie followed Rose down the ladder of the small plane and across the taxiway. They climbed the stairs and entered the airport building, housing four gates with the baggage claim in the center of the small building. From across the empty room, Stephanie spotted her brother standing at the baggage claim.

"Skip!" Racing to him, she leaped into his arms.

Rose's gaze followed Stephanie when the girl dashed to her brother. "Skip?" She jerked to a stop, shifting her gaze from the sweet little girl to her handsome big brother. "Oh, my word." Changing direction, she headed toward the baggage claim.

Stephanie clung to the good-looking lad, whose close resemblance indicated that they were indeed siblings, and the boy looked just like his father. That meant that Stephanie was her niece, and she never realized it.

"I missed you, Skip. Are you all right?" said Stephanie.

"I'm fine, but are you okay? Did they hurt you?"

Pulling her suitcase off the conveyor, Rose studied Skip. Dark glasses concealed a black eye, which had spread to his cheek.

"No, they didn't hurt me. But I was so scared. I didn't know when I would see you or Mom or my sisters again."

Skip embraced his little sister before gently setting her down. "Well, you're safe now. Let's go home."

Grasping his hand, Stephanie nodded.

"Stephanie, is this your brother?" asked Rose.

"Yes, ma'am. Skip, this is a nice lady that I met on the plane. She has the same name as me. Stephanie Rose."

"Pleased to meet you." Skip offered her his hand.

"It's a pleasure." Rose grasped his hand. "Oh, my, goodness! What happened to your wrist?"

"Rope burns. I got tangled up with a couple of guys that were more than I could handle."

"Hence, the black eye and bruised face."

"Is it that obvious?"

"Afraid so."

"How did they find you, Skip?" asked Stephanie. "I was so worried that those bad men would take me to Australia, and no one would find you."

Skip grinned. "They couldn't take you to Australia. You don't have a passport. And as for me, the Lord knew right where I was, and He showed the sheriff where to find me."

So Stephanie's account was factual, thought Rose. *Not fictional, as I originally thought.* "Skip, what's your last name?"

"Shaughnessy."

"And your father's name is Stephen?"

Skip grinned. "Yes, ma'am, how did you know that?"

"Is he well?"

"My father? He died four years ago."

Rose paled. "Died. Oh, no." Stunned, she slowly sat down.

Chapter 42

Wrapping up the Details

"Ma'am, are you all right?" Skip sat down beside her.

"Rose, what's the matter?" asked Stephanie. Taking the vacant chair next to Rose, Stephanie slid her arm around Rose's waist. "Rose?"

Gathering Stephanie into her arms, Rose held her close. "Stephanie, don't ever hold a grudge against your brother, like I did mine. I will never have another chance to show my brother how much I love him."

"Why not? I don't understand."

"You will." Rummaging through her purse, Rose pulled out a snapshot of a baby and handed it to Stephanie.

Stephanie grinned. "Oo, he's cute. Is this Robby?"

Taking the picture from Stephanie, Rose flipped it over. "No, sweetie. This is a picture of your brother."

Skip raised an eyebrow. On the back of the picture was written, "Skip Shaughnessy, one year old."

Turning to Skip, Rose handed him the photograph of his father. "Skip, you're the spitting image of your father." With a sorrowful sigh, she slipped the photographs back into her purse and looked at Stephanie. "I didn't even know that you were born. I missed out on so much because I held a grudge." Tears trailed down Rose's cheeks. "Your mom and dad named you after me."

Stephanie patted her shoulder while Rose blew her nose with a tissue fished from her purse.

Rose sighed. "Well, I guess I'll catch a hotel for the night and head back in the morning."

"But what about us?" cried Stephanie. "You haven't met our little sisters. Now that you know me and Skip, you have to meet everybody else."

"But I don't know your mother, my sister-in-law. We've never even met."

"Maybe it's time you do," said Skip. He stood and picked up her suitcase. "Why don't you come home with us? Mom would love to meet you."

"You really think so?"

"I know so."

Rose looked at Stephanie with wonder. "Stephen always said that he was going to name his daughter after me. Just knowing you children makes me feel close to him. Yes, I'll come with you."

"You folks finally ready to go?" asked the sheriff.

"I think so," said Skip, relieving Rose of her heavy suitcase.. "And we're bringing home one more. I hope Mabel and Woody don't mind."

"Are you kidding? Mabel thrives on having guests."

Taking Rose's hand, Stephanie followed Skip and Sheriff Robins out to the patrol car. The sheriff popped open the trunk before unlocking the doors.

"We're riding in a police car?" asked Rose.

"Yes, ma'am," said Skip. He opened the front door for her and the back door for his sister. Then he placed Rose's suitcase in the trunk of the squad car and closed the trunk.

Grasping her hand, Stephanie tugged her toward the car before scrambling into the back seat. "Ride in the back with me, Aunt Rose."

Rose glanced from the sheriff to Skip. The sheriff slid behind the wheel and started the car. Skip stood quietly at the back door, waiting for her to decide, but the sight of the cage made her nervous.

"Scoot over, Stephanie." Skip slid in beside her.

"I want my Aunt Rose to sit with me," said Stephanie. "Come on, Aunt Rose. It's great back here. I love to watch all the funny looks I get from people."

"Stephanie, you've ridden in the back seat of a police car before?"

"Lots of times. Come on."

Rose fidgeted outside the car. "All right. Just this once, but don't you dare tell anybody about this."

Skip slid out of the car and held the door while Rose crawled in beside Stephanie. After closing the rear car door, he scrambled in beside the sheriff, and they took off.

By the time the police cruiser pulled up to Woody's ranch house, it was nearly eight o'clock, and Skip could hardly keep his eyes open. He and the sheriff slid from the car and opened the rear doors for their passengers.

Rose slowly stepped from the squad car. "Skip, is this where you live?"

Skip retrieved Rose's suitcase from the back of the sheriff's car.

"No, ma'am. We're just visiting. Come, and I'll introduce you to everyone." Pulling the suitcase behind him, he pushed open the door and ushered the others in ahead of him.

"Skip, is that you?" called Woody from the dining room.

"Yes, sir."

Bolting from the kitchen, Cassandra flung her arms around his neck and kissed him. "I missed you." She cupped his face in her hands, examining his black eye and stroking his bruised cheek. "Are you okay? Uncle Woody told me everything."

"Everything?" Skip looked at Woody, who quickly shook his head. Planting his lips against Cassandra's, he said, "I'd like you to meet my dad's sister, Rose. Aunt Rose, this is my wife, Cassandra. We got married on Saturday."

"Three days ago?"

"Yes, ma'am. We're on our honeymoon."

Rose surveyed the room full of people. "You're teasing, right?"

Skip shook his head. "No, ma'am."

Starting with Woody, he introduced everyone. As the others broke into excited chatter, Skip drew Sheriff Robins aside. Escorting him around back to the small cabin, he retrieved the box of money he'd found at the farmhouse.

"Thanks, Skip. That young lady will be mighty happy when she sees this." The sheriff left, and Skip closed the door.

The house bustled with activity and noise while the cabin was peaceful and quiet. And right now, Skip treasured the solitude. Kicking off his shoes, he crawled onto the unmade bed and lay down, dropping into a sound sleep.

Cassandra pulled Stephanie into a hug. Tears of relief trickled down her cheeks. "I'm so sorry, Stephie. I never should have let you go into the farmhouse alone like that. Will you forgive me?"

Stephanie nodded. "Skip wouldn't like it if I got mad at you. He says that everyone makes mistakes."

"He's right."

The back door banged shut and Cassandra looked up to see Sheriff Robins enter the house with a gigantic book under his left arm.

"Ma'am, do you recognize this?" The sheriff showed it to Michelle.

The girl's mouth dropped open. "It's the box that my money was in."

"You'll be happy to know that it's still in here. I need to log this as evidence, and you'll get it back. Unfortunately, not until after the trial. And if we hope to get a conviction, we'll need your testimony."

"You've got it, said Michelle. "Is the money all there?"

"I don't know. Let's count it right now." Sitting on the sofa surrounded by witnesses, the sheriff counted the money.

Michelle sighed. "It's all there."

Rising, the sheriff closed the box and tucked it under his arm. "Well, folks. My job here is finished. I think I'll head home to get some sleep. Woody, is Dale staying with you folks?"

"Yeah. We were going to put the farm up for sale, but I've had second thoughts about it."

"So you're taking care of the Benson farm, then?"

Woody nodded.

"Good enough. Could I get you to stay out of the house for a couple of days? I want to take care of all of that stolen property first."

"Sure thing, Sheriff. Just let us know when you're through," said Woody.

"I'll do that. Good-bye, all. Miss Hunter, if you'll come out to the patrol car with me, I'll write you a receipt." Sheriff Robins waved as he hustled out the door.

Michelle followed him out, returning a minute later.

Woody collared her the moment she re-entered the house. "So what are your plans?"

"Well, I intend to talk to my sister to let her know that I recovered our money, even though it's currently not in my possession. Then I'm going to check in with my employer to see if I still have a job. If not, I'll put in some job applications. And I need to find my own apartment. Why do you ask?"

"I have a proposition for you. You need a place to stay, and the farm needs a caretaker. With Doug in prison and Dale staying with us, would you consider staying at the farm? You could take care of the animals and the house in exchange for the rent. If you should have any problems, you could call us."

"That would be wonderful. I'd love to. How long are we talking?"

"At least two years, until Dale's eighteen. Then, it would be up to him. What do you say?"

"What else can I say? Yes."

"Breakfast is ready," called Mabel. "Come and get it. Rose, you and Michelle grab plates and help yourselves."

"Where did Skip go?" asked Stephanie, looking around the room.

Cassandra surveyed the room, looking for him. Knowing he hadn't had much sleep the past few days, she knew he was tired. "He probably went to the cabin to rest. I need to check on him." Slipping out the back door, Cassandra hustled toward the little guest cabin.

Mabel darted after her. "Cassandra."

With her hand on the doorknob to the cabin, Cassandra grinned at her aunt. "Hi, Aunt Mabel. Did you want to talk to me?"

"Yes. I want you to know that Woody and I love having you kids, and you're always welcome here, but you and Skip need some time alone – just the two of you."

"What would you suggest?"

"At some point, Skip will take Rose and Stephanie to his house. You need to pack up and go along. Then after you drop off Rose and Stephanie, go somewhere by yourselves. That's what honeymoons are for."

Cassandra sighed at the pleasant thought of getting him alone. "Thanks, Aunt Mabel. We'll do that."

"Good. Woody and I will miss you, but you're doing the right thing. Now, breakfast is ready, so why don't you join us?

"I'll be right there."

Mabel left, and Cassandra quietly opened the door. Skip lay sound asleep on the bed, and she wasn't about to disturb him for breakfast. He could eat later.

When Skip awoke, he discovered that Cassandra had packed and left their suitcases sitting by the door.

Rubbing the sleep from his eyes, he slipped on his dark glasses and stepped out the door into the brilliant sunlight. Skip stifled a yawn and strolled down the walkway, entering the house through the backdoor. Following the sound of voices, he crossed the kitchen and exited through another doorway.

"We'll miss you, Cassandra," said Woody. "You and Skip, be sure to get back here. You did well. Your mother must be very pleased with your choice for a husband. Skip is the finest boy I've ever met. I'm delighted to call him my nephew."

"Skip's your nephew?" exclaimed Stephanie. "Then I'm your niece. That means you're my Uncle Woody, too."

Strolling into the living room, Skip quietly joined the others. Sometimes, he preferred to feel invisible, so it didn't bother him that no one acknowledged his presence.

Woody winked at Stephanie. "Stephie, you be a good girl for your mother and brother. I'd like to see you grow into a fine young lady."

"Yes, Uncle Woody. I will."

"Have a good nap, son?" asked Woody.

"Skip, you're up." Bounding to him, Cassandra flung her arms around his neck and kissed him.

"Are we leaving?" he asked.

"We need some time alone."

With a grin, Skip kissed her. "Yes, ma'am." Although he knew that he'd miss Mabel and Woody, the thought of spending time alone with Cassandra appealed to him.

A Way to Escape

Woody helped Skip haul the luggage out to his car and load it into the trunk, rearranging everything to make room for Stephanie's small suitcase and Rose's bags. Standing out by the car, everyone exchanged good-bye hugs and handshakes.

With teary eyes, Cassandra ran into Mabel's arms before giving her uncle a big hug.

Skip clasped Dale's hand. "Real pleasure to meet you, Dale. I'll be praying for you." Turning to Woody, Skip grasped his hand and drew him aside. "Thanks for everything, Woody. Please talk to Dale about his need for the Lord."

"You bet."

When he reached for Mabel's hand, she grabbed his wrist and pulled him into her arms. "Oh, no, you don't. I want a hug!" She embraced him tightly and kissed him on the cheek.

Cassandra burst into laughter. "I should have had my camera. What a sweet picture that would have made."

Skip's face got warm, and he grinned, unable to hide his embarrassment. "Bye, Aunt Mabel." Opening the car doors, he seated Cassandra in the front seat, while Rose and Stephanie climbed into the back. Skip cranked the engine and they took off.

"Be sure to come back for a visit," called Woody.

Once they were on the road, Rose pulled a deck of cards from her purse. "Stephanie, shall we play 'Go Fish?'"

"Oo, yes."

Skip drove in silence, listening to the giggling and game of cards going on behind him.

Cassandra reached over and touched his arm. "Skip, you never did agree to teach me how to drive."

"I'll teach you."

"When?"

"If you like, we'll start this afternoon. But first, you'll need a learner's permit, so you can drive legally."

"Skip, I want to go home," said Stephanie.

"I'm taking you home, Princess."

"Good, because I have so much to tell Mom. Honeymoons are really exciting. I can hardly wait to go on another one."

Skip and Cassandra exchanged glances and burst into laughter.

Your Eternity Awaits

Do You Know Jesus?

"For this is good and acceptable in the sight of God our Saviour;

Who will have all men to be saved, and to come unto the knowledge of the truth.

For there is one God, and one mediator between God and men, the man Christ Jesus."

I Timothy 2:3-5

Titus 2:11 says, **"For the grace of God that bringeth salvation hath appeared to all men."**

God is perfect, and He created mankind in His image. Adam and Eve, the first man and woman, were created in perfection. They were perfect because God their Creator is perfect. And because of God's holiness, He cannot have fellowship with sinful people.

So when Adam and Eve sinned, all of God's creation immediately fell into a sinful state, and all babies were born with a sinful nature.

Romans 5:12 says, **"Wherefore, as by one man sin entered into the world, and death by sin; and so death passed upon all men, for that all have sinned."**

As a result, we were separated from our holy Creator.

Romans 3:23 says, **"For all have sinned, and come short of the glory of God."**

Then Romans 6:23 says, **"For the wages of sin is death ..."**

Sin has a penalty – Death.

Everyone dies physically. That's the *first* death.

Revelation 20:14-15 says, **"And death and hell were cast into the lake of fire. This is the second death. And whosoever was not found written in the book of life was cast into the lake of fire."**

But God sent His Son to pay your penalty!

Romans 6:23 says, **"For the wages of sin is death; but the gift of God is eternal life through Jesus Christ our Lord."**

I Corinthians 15:3-4 says, **"For I delivered unto you first of all that which I also received, how that Christ died for our sins according to the scriptures; and that he was buried, and that he rose again the third day according to the scriptures."**

And God wishes none should perish. Not even you! So he made a way for you to escape eternal damnation in hell.

"For God so loved the world, that he gave his only begotten Son, that whosoever believeth in him should not perish, but have everlasting life." John 3:16

All You Have to do is Confess and Believe

Romans 10:9-10 says ...

"That if thou shalt confess with thy mouth the Lord Jesus, and shalt believe in thine heart that God hath raised him from the dead, thou shalt be saved.

For with the heart man believeth unto righteousness; and with the mouth, confession is made unto salvation."

Only those who accept Jesus as their Savior will have their names written in the Lamb's Book of Life. It's not a book of the names of every soul who's ever lived. No. It's God's *Book of Eternal Life,* containing the names of every soul who's trusted His Son as Savior.

But How Do I Get Saved?

1. Admit that you're a sinner and that you can't save yourself.

2. Believe in the Lord Jesus Christ

3. Confess and repent of your sins.

"For whosoever shall call upon the name of the Lord shall be saved." Romans 10:13

"And as it is appointed unto men once to die, but after this the judgment." Hebrews 9:27

Other Books Written by Marjorie Strebe

Skip Shaughnessy in Keeping Secrets

Book 1

When a rookie cop apprehends the drug dealer he believes is responsible for his dad's death, he's targeted by a drug gang who wants him dead, and he starts to fall in love with the adoring young girl whose father pulled the trigger.

Skip Shaughnessy in The Truth Shall Make You Free

Book 2

Two hours from home. In possession of fictitious ID. No one knows him.

On his way home from an undercover assignment, Skip stops to lend assistance to a couple of stranded teenage girls. When he's accidentally injured on their property, he wakes up in the massive estate owned by their father. No recollection of his identity or his past.

But despite amnesia, Skip has a way of influencing the lives of everyone he touches.

Treasures in My Spiritual Hope Chest
Volumes 1 & 2

A King James devotional book with scripturally-sound lessons to help you grow spiritually when you read, understand, and apply God's Word to your life. You will discover priceless nuggets of God's truth in each devotional.

Another, Day, Another Challenge:

The Biography of a Child with Williams Syndrome
Third Edition

A special needs child with a mental handicap and developmental delays is falling through the cracks of every service designed to support her needs.

Coming Soon

Skip Shaughnessy in The Troublemakers

His leave time is canceled. His honeymoon is cut short. He's pulling 16 hour duty days. And now he discovers that the troublemaker wreaking havoc in town is related to him.

For more information, visit www.marjiestrebe.com or email me at kjvwriter@marjiestrebe.com.